Praise for Linda Goodnight

"The second in the Buchanons series is a beautiful story that will surely leave readers feeling the holiday spirit."
—*RT Book Reviews* on *The Christmas Family*

"This is a heartfelt story with a sweet romance."
—*RT Book Reviews* on *The Lawman's Honor*

"A touching story that will renew the reader's holiday spirit."
—*RT Book Reviews* on *The Christmas Child*

Praise for Ruth Logan Herne

"Second chances and small-town charm combine in this final book in the Men of Allegany County series."
—*RT Book Reviews* on *Yuletide Hearts*

"A complicated and utterly compelling romance."
—*RT Book Reviews* on *Mended Hearts*

"Small-town charm abounds in Herne's characters and descriptions in this touching tale about finding strength in faith."
—*RT Book Reviews* on *The Mistletoe Family*

Linda Goodnight, a *New York Times* bestselling author and winner of a RITA® Award in inspirational fiction, has appeared on the Christian bestseller lists. Her novels have been translated into more than a dozen languages. Active in orphan ministry, Linda enjoys writing fiction that carries a message of hope in a sometimes dark world. She and her husband live in Oklahoma. Visit her website, lindagoodnight.com, for more information.

Multipublished bestselling author **Ruth Logan Herne** loves God, her country, her family, dogs, chocolate and coffee! Married to a very patient man, she lives in an old farmhouse in upstate New York and thinks possums should leave the cat food alone and snakes should always live outside. There are no exceptions to either rule! Visit Ruth at ruthloganherne.com.

A Cowboy Christmas

Linda Goodnight
and
Ruth Logan Herne

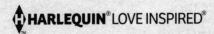

LOVE INSPIRED BOOKS

ISBN-13: 978-1-335-42848-6

A Cowboy Christmas

Copyright © 2018 by Harlequin Books S.A.

The publisher acknowledges the copyright holders of the individual works as follows:

Snowbound Christmas
Copyright © 2018 by Linda Goodnight

Falling for the Christmas Cowboy
Copyright © 2018 by Ruth M. Blodgett

www.Harlequin.com

Printed in U.S.A.

CONTENTS

SNOWBOUND CHRISTMAS   7
Linda Goodnight

FALLING FOR THE CHRISTMAS COWBOY   139
Ruth Logan Herne

SNOWBOUND
CHRISTMAS

Linda Goodnight

For the glory of Jesus, my Savior and King, that all might come to know You, and the forgiveness, peace and hope You freely give.

These things I have spoken unto you,
that in me ye might have peace. In the world
ye shall have tribulation: but be of good cheer;
I have overcome the world.
—*John* 16:33

Chapter One

Caleb Girard didn't believe in miracles. But he needed one.

With a frigid north wind ripping at him, Caleb kicked the wooden barn door closed and started toward his ranch house fifty yards away. The new calf shivered in his arms, a runt of a thing that wouldn't survive till morning in this weather. But Caleb was a man who believed in giving things a chance. Long ago, a man had given him the only chance he'd ever had, and now that man was dying.

Yeah. They needed a miracle. If Caleb was a praying man, he'd ask for one. But he'd never found praying to do one bit of good.

Sometimes God or life or whatever was unfair. But Pops, a devout Christian, would be brokenhearted to hear Caleb say such a thing. So he wouldn't. But he thought it. Every day since the terrifying diagnosis.

Chilled to the soul for more reasons than the arctic front, he stomped through the back door of the one-story house and placed the calf on a rug near the glowing fireplace. Ripley, his border collie, trotted in behind him and curled up beside the calf as if he knew the baby needed body heat.

Caleb gave the dog a gentle pat. "Take care of him, buddy."

He tossed another log on the fire and hung his coat on a peg by the door, anticipating an afternoon in the cold. If his rancher's intuition was right, snow would fall before Christmas. Or, worst-case scenario, ice. They got more of that in eastern Oklahoma than the fluffy stuff. Kids always hoped for snow. Realists and ranchers, of which he was both, appreciated the rain, but God could keep the rest.

He stopped at the kitchen sink to wash up. Maybe he'd put something in the Crock-Pot for supper. The old man's stomach had been iffy since this madness began. Some days he barely ate enough to nourish a guppy.

Drying his hands on a worn dish towel, Caleb walked down the short hall to Pops's bedroom. Next to the bed, Pops lay kicked back in his recliner, the farm-ranch report blaring from the flat-screen TV Caleb had hung on the wall a month ago. The older rancher raised a hand, his glassy eyes smiling at the man he'd called "son" for nearly seventeen years.

Greg Girard, the closest thing to a father Caleb had ever known, wasn't an old man. He was a sick one, a surprise that had knocked them both on their heels. How did a man go from seeming as fit as an Olympian to dying in two short months?

Caleb went to Pops's chair, feeling helpless and oversize in the presence of the once-robust man. "Think you can tolerate chili for supper tonight?" Maybe a stew would be better, though he'd fixed stew two nights ago. He was a serviceable cook but not a creative one.

"Sure. Whatever we got is fine with me."

"You say that every day." Then he'd barely pick at his meal.

"How's that cow? Calf here yet?"

"Had to pull the calf. Cow didn't make it."

Pops hissed through his teeth. "I knew we shouldn't have bought a bred heifer. Never can tell what kind of mama she'll make or what bull she's bred to."

But Pops was a soft touch and Billy Cloud had needed quick cash. Now the Girard ranch, which was only the two of them, was out the expense, the cow and maybe the calf.

"You're getting the short end of the stick lately, son, me lollygagging around so much."

"I got this, Pops. You take it easy."

"If I liked easy, I wouldn't have been a rancher." Pops gestured toward the machine a medical supply van had delivered earlier that day. "When're they coming to hook me up?"

"Didn't say."

Caleb went to the kitchen to mix up a bottle of colostrum replacer for the calf. Pops couldn't work more than an hour before fatigue overwhelmed him. He was gray as a winter day, nauseated more often than not, his legs swollen and weak. And he still thought he should get up every morning and head to the cow pastures.

As Caleb filled the calf's bottle, a knock at the door made him jump. He splashed liquid on his shirt.

With a growl of frustration, he went to the door, opened it.

And his belly dropped to the toes of his boots.

With frigid wind whipping her auburn ponytail like a wind sock, a woman stood on his porch. Kristen Andrews. Even bundled to her ears, he'd recognize her, though he hadn't seen her in years. What was she doing here?

Breathe, man. Breathe.

"You lost?" His voice sounded amazingly normal.

"Hi, Caleb. I'm freezing. May I come in?"

Before he'd barely stepped aside, she limped past him in a boot cast and entered his living room. He caught her fragrance, a mix of cold wind and coconut. She'd always smelled good, even when he'd worked so hard pretending not to notice.

Slim and pretty as ever, she shrugged out of a puffy white coat, draped it over the back of his favorite recliner and leveled a soft-eyed gaze in his direction. "How are you, Caleb?"

"Fine." *Except that my heart is trying to escape my rib cage.* "Yourself?"

"Great. Other than this broken leg." She motioned to the black boot.

He wanted to ask what had happened. Was that too nosy? Too intrusive? But she already knew he was an uncouth country bumpkin, so he asked anyway. "What happened?"

"Skiing accident a few weeks ago." She made a cute face that got his pulse pinging like a pinball. "I'm on the mend now that I'm home again."

She was back in Refuge? For good? He didn't know whether to shout hallelujah or break down and cry. It was so much easier to ignore her when he didn't run into her on the streets of small-town Oklahoma.

"Thought you were in Colorado."

"I was." Something shadowed her green eyes. She turned her head, swallowed, as if Colorado was a bad subject. He shouldn't have asked. "Where's our patient?"

It hit him then, right in the thick head. Blue scrubs. Medical bag. The nurse they were expecting was Kristen Andrews. He was going to be seeing her often. As in almost every day.

He hoped his heart could bear it.

It was ridiculous, really, Kristen mused as she and her cumbersome boot stumped behind Caleb to Greg Girard's bedroom.

She hadn't thought about Caleb in a long time, but as soon she'd received the doctor's orders to set up a care plan and home dialysis for Greg, Kristen had gone all fluttery. She'd told herself Caleb wouldn't be as attractive to an adult as he had been to a starry-eyed teenager. She'd been wrong.

She was practically engaged, but her pulse thudded like it had the first time she'd performed CPR in a code blue. The same as it had that one lovely day she'd spent alone with this particular cowboy years ago when she'd been convinced he was her forever and always. But after that one evening and one sizzling teenage kiss, he'd spent the rest of his senior year ignoring her. So she'd moved on, moved away and had almost forgotten the quiet boy with the sketchy background.

Intentionally putting aside thoughts of Caleb, she entered the sickroom. With a trained nose, she caught the scents of illness and identified them. Though shocked at the change in Greg Girard, she greeted him with her usual cheerful professionalism and kept her observations to herself.

As she directed Greg through his new care plan, emphasizing diet and fluid intake, Caleb hovered nearby, asking astute questions. Worry emanated from him. And, oddly, she was overly aware of his presence, of his outdoorsy scent, his wide shoulders, his trim form in old jeans. When their eyes collided, she locked in on the color. Gray and turbulent, like a winter's day.

"Doc says you can fix me up here at home," Greg was saying.

She tuned back in. Weird to be so aware of Caleb. "That's the plan. It will take several weeks, but you and Caleb can learn to use the machine yourselves."

"I don't know…" Caleb stepped closer to his dad's chair. "You sure about this, Pops? What if I mess up—"

Greg waved him off. "You won't."

"It's only natural to be anxious at first,"

Kristen assured him. "I'll work with you until you're confident."

Caleb looked as if the idea gave him indigestion. "Great."

Was that a "good" *great* or a sarcastic one?

He spun on his cowboy boots. "I'll be in the kitchen."

She turned her attention to Greg, but Caleb's unfriendly behavior stung.

Yet the teenage Caleb had barely given her the time of day. Why would she expect the adult version to be any different? He was her brothers' pal, and she was the annoying little sister. If she really knew him, he'd probably be as big a disappointment as Dr. Dud.

The sore spot in her heart throbbed. James Dudley, a bright, charming and successful cardiologist who loved outdoors and her—she'd thought. He was everything she was looking for in a man. Until the ski trip. She kept expecting him to call, apologize and pick up where they'd left off. He hadn't.

Kristen turned her focus to Greg's vital signs and physical assessment, jotting notes as she worked.

When she finished, she returned the blood pressure monitor to her nursing bag.

"How's it sound?" Greg asked with a crooked half smile.

"A little out of whack." She winked. "Let's get that machine fired up and get your dialysis going. Then everything will look better."

"That's what they keep telling me." He twisted in his chair. "Caleb!"

The other cowboy appeared immediately, a giant baby bottle in one hand. "What is it, Pops? Need something?"

"Kristen's about to crank up R2-D2. You gonna watch?"

Kristen laughed. "R2-D2?"

"Sure. Look at that thing. Don't you watch *Star Wars*?"

The look Caleb gave his dad was amused and tender. "Let me put this up and wash my hands."

Caleb hated this. Hated the fear, hated the disease, hated seeing Pops's blood flowing out of his body and into a machine.

Somehow Pops put on a happy face and chatted up Kristen as if she hadn't been gone for six or seven years. Caleb felt like a voyeur as he listened in on the conversation, snatching up bits of personal information about the girl he'd never forgotten.

That she was a registered nurse with advanced training didn't surprise him. He'd known she went off to some big college in Colorado on a scholarship. She was smart, classy, a sweet-natured girl who was nice to everyone. Like him. Even though he'd been a troubled foster kid nobody but Pops wanted, she'd acted as if he was every bit as good as her preppy friends.

Then she'd left Refuge for college and stayed away, a surprise, given her great family. She and her family had always been close. A normal family, like the one he'd never had. He'd envied her and her brothers for that. Probably one of the reasons he'd hung around her house so often. That and his mad crush on Kristen.

"Watch both wounds for signs of infection," she was saying.

Caleb tuned in, loving the sound of her voice. Educated, but not haughty about it. He liked watching her mouth move, too. She had a soft, kissable mouth, as he well remembered. That kiss had haunted him. Haunted him still.

"What are the signs?" he managed to ask when his brain settled back down.

"I'll leave you a list but, in general, call me if you notice anything unusual around either site. Or if he runs a fever." She pointed to the place where two tubes entered Pops's forearm. "The fistula takes a while to heal."

He nodded, knowing he was in over his head but trying to appear halfway intelligent. "The doc told us. Pops has the chest catheter for now. Until the fistula heals."

The wound in his dad's forearm gave him the creeps. The idea that a thick vessel would develop under Pops's skin like a gopher tunnel was one he didn't like to think about. But if it kept Pops alive, Caleb didn't care if it was as big as the Holland Tunnel.

"Healing could take several months," she said.

Months of watching Pops suffer, watching him deteriorate daily. Yesterday he'd been too weak and short of breath to saddle a horse.

Caleb squeezed the bridge of his nose, wishing he could turn back the clock. For months, maybe longer, Pops had been sick and hadn't known it. And even when the symptoms hit, he'd ignored them too long. The cowboy way. Suck it up, be tough, keep going.

Kristen went through a few more instructions, using big words and then dumbing them down for him and Pops. Caleb's head hurt from information overload.

Eventually, Pops waved them away. "You two go somewhere else so I can catch a nap."

Kristen patted his shoulder. "I can't go far. Maybe the living room. I'll tiptoe in occasionally to check your monitors. You get that two-hour snooze."

Pops gave her a grin and a wink. If Caleb didn't know better, he'd say the old man was flirting.

He turned and went back to the living room

to finish feeding the calf, aware that Kristen followed. At Caleb's entrance, Ripley whopped his tail against the rug.

Caleb dropped a hand to the black-and-white head. "Hey, Rip, looking after the baby?"

"Rip?" Kristen approached with caution, standing behind Caleb's shoulder, close enough to brush his arm. "As in he'll rip my throat out?"

He was so aware of her, his skin tingled. "As in Ripley, which sounds too grand for a working cow dog. Rip for short."

"Won't he hurt the calf?"

"Nope. He'll protect her."

To prove as much, Ripley began licking the calf's still-damp forehead. Gently, Caleb eased him aside and urged the calf onto her wobbly legs to recommence the feeding regimen.

Rip curled into a circle at Caleb's feet to watch.

"What happened to his mama?" Kristen settled on the couch almost close enough to touch, an electronic tablet on her lap.

"Calf's a her. A heifer." As if the calf knew they were speaking about her, she gave the bottle several hard head butts. "Feisty girl to be so little, but her size may have saved her life. She had a leg turned back and under. Couldn't deliver. Cow died."

"Poor little orphan."

The term caused a burn in the pit of Caleb's

stomach. He'd been a social orphan, not a biological one, but either way, he'd been without a parent. Like this calf. "I'll take care of her."

Like Pops had done for him. Like Caleb tried to do with the group of boys he mentored.

"Will she survive?"

"Hopefully. This colostrum will help. Sometimes I don't find the calves quick enough."

"Colostrum is important in humans, too."

"I guess you'd know about that. For cattle, we've got about six hours before the gut will no longer absorb these essential nutrients, so the quicker I get this in her, the better."

"You must have to know a lot to care for cattle."

Nothing like what a college-educated nurse had to know to care for people. "We do what we can. If that means letting a calf sleep in my living room, I'm willing."

"You were always a kind person."

The comment caught him off guard. "I was?"

"Remember that kid in high school with the speech impediment?"

"Jimmy Starks." He hadn't thought about the poor stuttering kid in years.

"You punched Trent White for tormenting him."

Caleb snorted. "And got suspended."

"You shouldn't have. Trent was a bully before bullying was a thing."

"Bullying was always a thing, Kristen." She'd just been too popular to be the object. Right side of the tracks, good Christian family with a respected mother and a successful father, smart and pretty Kristen had it all.

If Caleb hadn't learned to hit first and apologize later, he'd have been more tormented than poor Jimmy. *Foster boy, dummy, loser, who's your daddy?* Those were only a few of the remarks he'd endured. They'd made him feel as worthless as used tissue. As a result, he'd hated school. And his grades had shown it.

Kristen tapped the iPad a few more times and then went to check on Pops. Her boot cast thudded on the wooden floor, warning him of her going and coming. Again, he wanted to ask about the accident. This time, he didn't. He didn't want her scowling at him again.

When she returned, she came to the fireplace, where he was stroking the calf's neck to encourage her to swallow. The flames flickered behind her, yellow and blue and warm.

He looked up at her. "Pops doing all right?"

She stretched her hands behind her back, toward the fire. "Sleeping."

"He does that a lot."

"He needs a transplant," she said softly.

"I know that." His tone was harsh. "He's on the registry."

She perched on the raised brick hearth, watching him with sympathy. "I'm sorry. This has to be incredibly difficult for you."

"Not for me. For him." He didn't matter. Pops did. "I'd give him both my kidneys if they'd match."

She smiled a sad smile. "All it takes is one."

"Which we can't find." Fury at the injustice boiled in his gut. "Probably won't find. Not with his rare antibody."

"He's a tough match, but not impossible."

"How long can he live like this without a transplant?"

Her eyes shifted. She grew wary. She picked imaginary lint from her blue scrub pants. "Statistics vary, and averages don't consider the individual. Your dad doesn't have some of the other risk factors, so with dialysis, he could live a long time."

Or he could die tomorrow. That was what she wasn't saying.

The calf drained the bottle, and Caleb lowered the animal to the rug and went into the kitchen. At the sink, he washed out the container, his heart heavy as a boulder. He was a man of action, a man who took charge of his sick animals and found a way to make them well. That he couldn't do the same for Pops made him crazy.

Chapter Two

Caleb carried her bag to the car. Kristen had been mildly amused that he'd held her elbow while she'd thumped like a flat tire in her boot cast down the incline from his porch to her car. The leg was healing. She was an independent adult who could manage alone. But there was something to be said for a thoughtful man.

He'd even opened her car door and waited in the December cold, hands shoved in his jeans pockets, for her and her bum leg to settle in.

"See you tomorrow," she said, putting on her seat belt.

Caleb leaned in, one hand on top of the Honda. "Same time?"

Their gazes met, and Kristen experienced that disconcerting flutter again. "If not, I'll give you a call."

"Okay. Thanks." He closed the door and stepped

back, watching as she took off. When she glanced in her mirror, he still stood there, wind stirring his brown hair, his olive flannel shirt plastered against his body. He looked incredibly alone.

Like she'd felt the day James had left.

Eyes were the windows to the soul, and Caleb Girard's said he was sick with fear and sadness. Anger, too. As a nurse, she recognized the normal progression of emotions in life-and-death situations. As a woman who'd once adored him, she ached for his aloneness and despair.

There had to be more they could do to procure a kidney for Greg. Thousands died every year waiting for a transplant. She hadn't told this gruesome statistic to Caleb or Greg. Hope was essential. Greg had it. Caleb was struggling.

After a stop at the Refuge Home Health office, Kristen visited one more patient, who needed an IV infusion, before calling it a day. That done, she stopped at her childhood home. Dad wasn't yet home from his real estate office, but Mom was. After twenty-six years of working alongside Dad, Evie Andrews was semiretired, showing homes only when she wanted to.

A honey blonde carrying a few extra pounds, Evie greeted Kristen with a hug. "There you are. Staying for dinner, I hope. I have lemon chicken in the oven."

"One of my favorites, as you well know."

Mom offered a guilty shoulder shrug. "Funny how that worked out."

Grinning, Kristen limped through the tidy living room where she'd grown up, past Mom's perfectly decorated, lit Christmas tree, to the island separating the living area from the kitchen. She climbed onto a bar stool and propped her boot on the rung of another.

"Your leg doing okay now that you're working again?"

"It's tired at the end of the day, but I'm not having any pain to speak of."

"Which you wouldn't speak of even if you were in agony." Mom moved around the island to the stove. "Cup of tea?"

"Sounds wonderful. But I can make it." Kristen started to rise.

"Sit. Let me pretend you still need me."

"Oh, Mama, I'll always need you."

Her mother set the kettle to heat. "Still haven't heard from Dr. Dudley?"

An ache pulsed in Kristen's chest. "I thought he'd call by now, wanting to make up."

"But he hasn't?"

"Not even a text to inquire about the fractured fibula."

"I know he's a busy physician, but common courtesy demands at least a phone call." Evie opened a cabinet. "Maybe he's not as great as we thought."

Maybe he wasn't.

She'd thought she was in love with him. Wanted to be in love. Biology didn't wait forever, and she wanted children, though she hadn't mentioned kids to James. Not yet anyway. She'd assumed he'd feel the same. After his behavior at the ski lodge, and his cold silence since, she wasn't sure of anything.

Her mom slid a steaming cup of Earl Grey in front of her. "How's Greg Girard doing?"

Cup at her lips, Kristen blinked at her mother. "How did you know I was at his ranch today?"

"Sugar, this is Refuge, not Denver. Remember how you and your brothers used to get so aggravated because Dad and I knew what you'd been up to before you could tell us."

"That *was* annoying. Like the time I was nominated for homecoming queen. I was so excited to tell you."

"But Shawna Rich told us first."

"I'm still mad at her about that."

They both laughed, knowing she joked. She and Shawna remained close friends.

"So, how is Greg?" Evie leaned both elbows on the island.

Kristen shook her head. "Patient confidentiality, Mom."

Her mom made a face. "Which doesn't mean beans in Refuge. Greg's in our discipleship class at church. We know he's in kidney failure. Everyone does. As soon as he received the diagnosis, he called your dad, asking for the class to pray."

There were few secrets in Refuge, especially when someone was ill. "Greg is upbeat, as usual, trying to be positive, but frankly, he needs a miracle."

"Someone somewhere has to be a donor match."

"Finding that person is the problem." She didn't go into the sad statistics. She was a woman of science, but she and her family were also people of faith. "Sometimes it's hard to trust that God will do whatever's best, even if His idea of 'best' is not what we hoped."

"I know, sweetie. I know. I feel as bad for Caleb as I do Greg. Maybe worse. Greg is the only family he has. We know where Greg is going if he loses this battle, but Caleb will be lost without his anchor."

"He seems scared and worried, though he wouldn't ever admit as much. Cowboy tough, all the way. But he's trying hard to take care of his dad."

"He was always a good boy under that nobody's-gonna-hurt-me-again reserve. I liked him. And if my memory serves, you liked him, too. You were always tagging around after your brothers whenever they brought Caleb home."

Kristen rolled her eyes upward. "Was I really that obvious?"

"Uh-huh. Starry-eyed teenage crushes, we all go through them."

Caleb had probably thought she was a silly goose. But they were grown-ups now and teenage crushes had given way to more meaningful relationships. She wondered why Caleb wasn't married.

"You know what's sad?" Lifting the boot, she swiveled the bar stool toward the lit Christmas tree. "There wasn't one sign of Christmas in that house."

"I guess Greg's not up to it."

"Maybe they don't decorate, being single guys and all. But that's sad to me."

"Some don't. It bothers you because you're a Christmas-cookie kind of girl with all the trimmings." Evie dipped her tea bag up and down in the cup. "Which reminds me. Want to come over next week and bake pumpkin bread for the neighbors? It'll be like old times, when you were in high school and we baked for your teachers."

"And the fire department and police officers." She set her tea on the speckled gray granite. "I loved doing that. Refuge has such a great community."

Refuge *was* a great community, filled with caring people.

An idea popped into Kristen's head. One she couldn't wait to share with Caleb.

Caleb thought she was the cutest female buzz saw he'd ever seen. Being a cautious man, he kept the thought to himself. He grinned a little, though, when Kristen plopped onto a kitchen chair, pen and paper in hand, black boot sticking straight out, and declared her plan to find a kidney for Pops.

She'd already hooked Pops to R2-D2, forcing both men to watch, listen and repeat every step. Kristen was a good teacher, but an exacting one. He appreciated that even if it surprised him. *Do it. Do it right.* Pops's life depended on it.

"Help me make a list." She tapped the pen against her chin.

"A list of what? People who might donate?" Rip ambled in from Pops's room and stood beside Caleb's chair, quiet and polite. He appreciated that in a dog, a horse, too.

"Civic groups, churches and, yes, specific people if you can think of any."

He couldn't. "None that I haven't already asked."

"All right, then, let's brainstorm groups to speak to."

"Speak to? As in talk in front of people?" He dropped a hand to Rip's head.

She snickered. "Scared?"

Terrified, but he wouldn't admit it. "I'm not a good speaker. I barely talk to individuals. Cows and horses, yes. Groups of people, no."

People stared and judged, and he was certain he'd make a fool of himself and ruin Pops's chances. He didn't have the education or the vocabulary to be a speaker.

"I think you'd be great," she said, "but if it makes you feel better, I'll handle most of the speaking. You come along to put a face to the need."

He could do that. Fact was, he'd do anything. And the little perverse imp on his shoulder loved the idea of spending extra time with Kristen. The smart part of his brain knew better. "Whatever it takes."

She gave him the kind of smile that made a man want to do anything she asked. "That's the spirit. The more we raise awareness, the more opportunity we have of seeing the right donor step up."

Caleb was skeptical, but he admired Kristen's spunk, her determination, her sheer faith that they would succeed. Even if it all turned out to be a wasted effort, they'd know they tried.

They spent the next twenty minutes brainstorming places to speak and social media, all of which Pops would have to approve. Then, after a check of Pops's machinery, Kristen started looking up numbers on her cell phone.

"Here," he said, holding out a hand. "Give me half the list. I can look up numbers."

"As long as you don't have to talk to them?"

He gave her a scowl. "I can call. But they'll respond better to you."

"What makes you think that? I'm the one who's been gone for a long time. They probably won't remember me."

Oh, they'd remember her, all right. Kristen Andrews of the auburn hair, sea green eyes and big, big heart was unforgettable. Whether or not anyone would line up to give away a kidney at her request? That was the part that worried him.

Chapter Three

Caleb stared at the sea of faces gathered in the meeting room of the Refuge Library. They made him nervous. So much so that he'd twisted the brim of his hat into a knot. He was nervous for Kristen, nervous for Greg, nervous that no one would even care about one old rancher with dead kidneys and no family other than an adopted son whose blood type didn't even match.

Members of a local service club listened with varying amounts of interest. From his place on the dais, Caleb could see their faces and the few who played on their cell phones while Kristen explained the life-and-death scenarios people like his dad lived with every day.

He wanted to get up and punch the cell phone users, demand they listen and care. Kristen was terrific. Articulate, warm, funny. And the PowerPoint presentation was an attention grabber filled with grim facts as well as the hope and long life that could be realized through a living kidney donation. He was learning from her, too.

When she introduced Caleb, he stood, awkward as a three-legged calf. *Here goes nothing*, he thought for the sixth time in two weeks. He was the face of the issue, like he'd been years ago on one of those news programs that beg people to adopt older kids. He remembered the humiliation, the feeling that he was a germ under the microscope and lesser somehow because he had no parents to love him.

This was different, though. This wasn't about him. This was about Greg, the only person to respond to that long-ago news program. As long as he could remember that, he didn't care if his face was hotter than a brush fire or that his knees wobbled like Jell-O.

He stepped up to the microphone, cleared his throat and read from the paper he'd written and rewritten.

"Pops. That's my dad," he started, feeling proud as he always did to be able to claim Greg Girard as his dad. "He's the best man I know, a hard worker, a real cowboy who loves his neighbor like the Good Book says and goes the extra mile to help others. He used to donate blood every time the mobile came to town, and after fire wiped out the Belgers' hay barn, he fed their cows all through the winter out of our barn, free of charge. We ran a little short that spring, but he never mentioned the reason, just went to the feed store and bought expensive feed."

Though his fingers trembled, he peeked at the crowd. Most were listening. He looked back at his notes.

"Even after his kidneys failed and he had to go on dialysis or die, he was thinking about others. At Thanksgiving, he drove around Refuge, distributing beef from our herd to families who were having a hard time. I could tell you lots of stories about him like that, but I'll just leave you with this thought. If it was your dad, wouldn't you want someone to step up and save his life?"

Grabbing his hat, he sat down again. Blood pulsed in his head. He had no memory of what he'd said. He hoped he'd made sense. He twisted his hat again, aware he was about to ruin a perfectly good Resistol.

Kristen turned her head, gave him one of her reassuring smiles, the kind that lit him up on the inside, fool that he was. She always said he did great. He doubted it. She was nice like that.

They were, however, making progress. Thanks to her. Every time they did this speaking gig, several attendees took the business cards he'd had printed with the donation center's information.

Each response, small though it was, gave him

hope. Not much, but enough to keep him rushing through chores to meet Kristen at the Lions Club or the arts council or any of number of churches who'd agreed to hear them speak.

When her talk ended, followed by polite applause, the group took a break, and he found himself uncomfortably surrounded with questioners. He looked for Kristen, but as happened every time, she was surrounded, too.

"Why don't *you* give your dad a kidney?" The man in a yellow golf shirt seemed almost accusatory.

"I'm not a match. He's type O. I'm AB. His donor needs to be O."

A woman with a kind face asked from behind purple glasses, "I know your dad. How's he doing?"

"Holding his own, thank you. But like Kristen mentioned on the PowerPoint, being on dialysis a long time shortens his life span, even after he gets a new kidney. We need a donor as soon as possible."

Somehow he got through the rest of the questions and wove his way past clutches of conversations toward Kristen. She was the real power behind this campaign, and every time they were together, he found himself more and more captivated by her.

The wild teenage love he'd suffered in high

school had grown up to be every bit as wild. His certainty that he didn't stand a chance with her was even wilder. Love her from afar, but keep his mouth shut. That was his modus operandi.

He spotted her then, as questioners drifted away, leaving one gray-suited man and Kristen. The man was standing a little too close, Caleb thought. Kristen stepped back two paces and ended up against a wall. The man followed, talking, his hands gesturing. Caleb recognized him.

Danny Bert. Used-car salesman. High school jock and bully.

Something dark moved inside Caleb, a primal sense of protectiveness. He picked up his pace, excusing himself as he brushed past the remaining people.

"You haven't been around in a while, Kristen," the suit was saying. "Maybe we should have coffee and talk over old times and this donor thing. I know a great little place that stays open late."

"Sorry, Danny, I can't, but I appreciate your interest in donating. Call the number on the card, and they'll get you started."

"I'd rather talk to you. Old times and all. Remember the junior prom? You and me. It might be worth that phone call you want me to make. Quid pro quo?"

Caleb didn't like the sound of those words. Whatever they meant.

Kristen crossed her arms. Conflicting emotions flashed on her face. She didn't want to turn away a possible donor, but Danny was coming on too strong. That he was a man accustomed to having his way was no secret to anyone in Refuge.

Caleb stepped in next to Kristen, ignoring the car salesman. "Ready to go? I could use that Coke you promised me."

"Oh, there you are." Relief smoothed the frown between her eyes. She relaxed her arms. "Yes, I'm ready. Let me grab the laptop first."

"Sure thing." He slipped an arm around Kristen's waist, hoping Danny picked up on the subtle clues. Hoping even more that Kristen wouldn't slap him silly.

Danny looked from him to Kristen. "You're with him?"

The way the car salesman said *him* prickled the hair on the back of Caleb's neck. He'd heard that tone before. Danny treated him like a speck of manure on the bottom of his shoe. Always had.

Maybe he was, but Kristen wasn't.

For good measure, he shoulder jostled the former jock and left him standing there.

"I could have handled him," Kristen said when they reached the dais.

The meeting room emptied, including Danny

Bert, who was busy schmoozing someone else by the time he reached the exit. Probably selling the man a car. Or a beachfront property in Arizona.

"I know you could." He closed the laptop, figuring she was mad now. "Sorry if I overstepped."

"You didn't. Thank you. Danny has always been pushy."

"Yeah."

She gathered her notes and stuck them in a tote. "I owe you that Coke."

His head jerked up. "I just said that to—"

She put a hand on his arm. "I know. But a Coke sounds good after all that talking."

"Pops might need me."

"Your dad is at Bible study."

"Oh." He knew that. He hadn't expected her to.

He shouldn't go with her. They already spent so much time together he could barely think straight.

But he was a weak man. Slapping his hat on his head, he asked, "Where to?"

Kristen was chiding herself as she slid into the booth at the fast-food restaurant. Caleb had been sweet to rescue her from that irritant Danny Bert, but he hadn't wanted to come here and extend their time together. Why had she insisted?

And what was it about her that found aloof men so intriguing?

Caleb set a lidded fountain drink in front of her and slid in on the other side of the booth. His foot jostled her boot cast.

"Sorry. Did that hurt?" He gripped his soda cup until she thought he'd pop the lid off.

"Not at all."

His fingers eased their stranglehold. "When do you get free of the boot?"

"Another week, I hope. I'm healing faster than expected."

She sipped at the Coke, remembering the only other time she and Caleb had shared a soda in this place. Maybe in this exact booth. "Tonight went great, I thought. I gave out ten cards."

"About the same for me."

"They won't all follow through, but maybe some will."

"Like Danny Bert?"

She rolled her eyes. "Danny's a wart on the world."

Caleb laughed, coughed, choked on his drink.

She handed him a napkin, chuckling. "It isn't very Christian of me, but ever since I was his date to the junior prom, he thinks I owe him something."

Caleb's eyes danced. "Corsages are pricey."

"Why, Mr. Girard, are you making fun of me?"

"Depends on how much you liked the flowers, I guess. I didn't go to the junior prom."

"Or the senior one, either." A blush crept up her neck. Why had she said that? It was ages ago, and that she remembered seemed...pathetic.

"Nope. Neither one." He pumped his straw up and down in the lid without drinking. "I was never much for dancing."

"I thought all cowboys could scoot a boot."

"Nah." His mouth curved. "That's only in the movies. All my boot scooting happens when a bull gets after me."

Kristen laughed. "A regular twinkle toes?"

"Something like that." He sipped from the straw. "You hungry? I was thinking some fries sound good."

"I normally don't eat fast food, but you go ahead."

He scooted out of the booth, and she watched him walk to the counter. He wasn't a swaggering cowboy, but he sure looked good in jeans and cowboy boots.

A dozen emotions flooded through Caleb as he carried his order back to the booth. He should hit the trail, forget the food, forget Kristen Andrews.

He doubted she remembered the only other time they'd been in this restaurant together, but he remembered. She'd been sixteen, a bouncy cheerleader in white shorts and a green shirt, cute and friendly as a pup. He'd fallen so in love with her, he hadn't slept at all that night.

He slid the tray onto the table and sat again. They were adults now, so why couldn't his heart behave like one?

He'd barely settled when she pinned him with those green eyes. "Why aren't you married, Caleb?"

A dozen reasons. He came from bad blood. He didn't know how to be a husband. He sure didn't know how to be a father. He'd decided long ago to remain a bachelor like Pops.

"No one will have me," he joked.

"Oh, come on." She tapped his fingers like a schoolmarm with a ruler. "Be serious. Haven't you ever been in love?"

"Once." And once was all it took. "I decided the whole marriage and family thing wasn't for me. You?"

"I've thought so a couple of times."

His heart squeezed. "But?"

"Things haven't worked out. Yet. I'm still praying and asking for God's direction." She pulled the straw loose from the lid and studied the drippy end. "I'd like to get married someday and have a family, the way my parents did."

An all-American, traditional family like hers. He couldn't begin to fathom what that was like.

"Must have been some smart man in Colorado who caught your eye."

"There was."

"But not anymore?" A zing of hope shot up like a July thermometer.

"Not sure. We're…taking a break. His practice is really busy."

He didn't care how busy he was. If Kristen was his woman, he'd find time. "Practice? He a lawyer?"

"James is a doctor. A surgeon."

Hoped faded, crashed, ached.

James. A doctor. Smart and successful. And probably rich. Exactly the kind of man Kristen deserved.

Another reason Caleb would remain a bachelor.

Chapter Four

"You're going out to see that cute cowboy again?" Kristen's coworker Trina stepped into the supply room inside the home health office, where Kristen gathered the supplies for another trip to the Girard ranch.

Kristen dropped dialysis tubing into her bag and reached for the wound-care supplies. Because his treatment took several hours, she saved Greg Girard's visit for last.

"Which cute cowboy would that be?" She knew full well which one. Caleb was seldom far from her thoughts.

Something had changed between her and Caleb that late night over french fries and soda refills. She didn't know what it was. She wasn't a lovesick teenager anymore, but she couldn't deny the powerful pull between her and the cowboy. So powerful in fact, that she wanted closure with James. Not that she and Caleb were an item, but spending time with the cowboy had cleared the fog from her brain. She wasn't in love with James. And he certainly hadn't been in love with her. He'd wanted her, yes, but love and respect? Not even close.

She thanked God He'd opened her eyes to that truth before it was too late.

Trina reached for the irrigation syringes. "Caleb Girard is one of the most eligible and best-looking bachelors in Refuge. All that cowboy charisma is yummy."

Chemistry and biology. Exactly. The fact that her nerve endings tingled whenever Caleb entered the house was a simple case of attractive male and single female on the rebound. Instant appeal. At least on her part. "Even if I did have my eye on him, Caleb isn't interested in me."

If they so much as brushed arms in the hallway, he jumped like she'd hit him with a defibrillator.

Look, but don't get close was the message she received.

"He's not interested in anyone from what I've noticed. And trust me, I've noticed. He rarely dates."

Kristen had noticed, too.

"True. He's not real social. Kind of shy, I think. Plus, running a ranch is hard, endless work. With his dad unable to contribute as much as he used to, all the chores fall on Caleb's shoulders."

Caleb would tromp into the house, ice frozen on his hair or soaking wet from rain, dutifully receive his dialysis lesson while he warmed up, talk a bit about the cows or horses or a red fox he'd seen and then head back out into the December cold.

She looked forward to those brief conversations as well as to the evenings they spent recruiting donors. They made a good team.

"Sounds like you're admiring someone," Trina said in a singsong voice, teasing.

"I *do* admire him. You should see him with his dad. It's kind of heartrending, but tender and sweet, too. He's desperate to make Greg well, as if he has that power."

"Poor guy. Must be tough."

"When we speak to groups about kidney donation, he visibly shakes. He hates being the center of attention, but he gets up there anyway." And looked mighty fine doing it. A white shirt, well-pressed jeans and that black cowboy hat on a handsome man could give any woman cardiac arrhythmia.

Trina slipped a stack of medical forms onto a clipboard. "Sounds like a catch to me. Caring, thoughtful guy. Easy on the eyes. Kind of lonely and shy. You'd be doing him a favor to ask him out."

Kristen shook her head and forced out a laugh as she slipped on her coat. Caleb *was* a catch. But, after the fiasco with James, she'd stick with friendship for now.

Friendship was less risky.

Kristen was here.

Caleb's belly lifted and dropped like it did when he took a hill too fast in his pickup truck.

Cloaked to the ears in the white quilted coat with a green plaid scarf around her neck, the woman he couldn't get out of his mind walked into his house, toting a pot of red flowers and a white paper sack.

She couldn't possibly know about today. Unless Pops had told her. "What's the occasion?"

"Christmas. These are poinsettias." She handed him the flowers and the sack and began unwinding her scarf. "And some good news."

His pulse jumped. "A donor?"

"Not yet, but we're getting closer." She took the white sack from him and went into the kitchen. That was Kristen, comfortable with people in a way he wasn't. "The donation center says twenty-seven people have signed up to be tested for Greg since we started our awareness campaign."

She looked so right in his house, he had the completely inappropriate longing to pull her close, the way a husband would greet a wife.

Instead, he shoved the idea as far back in his head as it would go—which wasn't far enough—and set the potted plant on the bar between them. It was pretty. Brightened up the place. Like she did.

"Hear that, Pops?" he called toward the back of the house.

"Sure did." Pops exited the laundry room, a basket in his arms. Caleb took it. Pops scowled but didn't argue.

"I'm praying one of them is right for you," Kristen said.

"Hard as it is to covet another man's property," Pops said, "I'm praying with you."

Talk of prayer made Caleb fidgety. He'd tried it lately. Hadn't done much good.

He put the thought on pause and frowned. Could God be responsible for the twenty-seven sign-ups?

Kristen removed a plate from the cabinet and arranged some Christmas cookies and perky gingerbread men in a pretty circle. He and Pops never got that fancy. They ate right out of the sack.

"You brought cookies?" he asked.

"I thought a celebration was in order."

"It sure is." Pops shot him a grin.

"Pops," Caleb warned with a shake of his head.

The ornery old cowboy chuckled. "Oh, quit bellyaching. Every man gets older once a year. This little lady brought you flowers and cookies. Enjoy 'em."

Caleb was watching Kristen's face and saw when she caught on to Pops's not-so-subtle hints.

"Today is your birthday? Why didn't you tell me?" Her eyes lit up like candles on a cake. She circled the end of the bar and threw her arms around him. "Happy birthday!"

She smelled like sugar cookies and felt so right in his arms, he wanted to stand there for an hour. Made a man want to have a birthday every day, though his was nothing much to celebrate.

The snotty little imp in his head piped up. Kristen was taken. A doctor boyfriend. She was a people person, a hugger. Hugging meant exactly nothing.

His sneaky hands slid around her anyway. When the moment ended, he wanted to tell her it was the best birthday gift of his life. But that might hurt Pops's feelings and make Kristen uncomfortable. Like Caleb was now.

"If I'd known, I'd have brought a birthday cake instead." Her green eyes sparkled like jewels in sunlight. That was Kristen, sunny and warm on a cold, dark day.

"Aw, it's no big deal. Cookies are great."

"Of course it's a big deal. At my house, Mom still bakes a cake and invites the whole family." She roofed her hands over her head. "Then she makes us all wear those ridiculous pointed hats and leis. And the birthday boy or girl wears this huge flashing button that says, 'Hug me. It's my birthday.'"

Her family birthdays sounded amazing. He couldn't fathom that, either.

Pops, whose eyes sparkled as much as Kristen's, couldn't let well enough alone. "Us old bachelors don't know much about birthday partying. So what say you stick around after my date with R2-D2 and show us how it's done?"

"Pops, Kristen's worked all day."

"Which means she's gotta be hungrier than a toothless coyote in a lettuce factory. Why don't you whip us up a steak while she and I visit our mechanical pal?" To Kristen, Pops said, "You wouldn't turn down a sick old man on his son's birthday, now would you?"

Pops had their guest between a rock and a boulder. She might not want to stay for dinner, but she was too kind to reject such a pitiful plea.

Every cell in Caleb's stupid body was thrilled when she agreed.

* * *

The next morning was as cold as Antarctica but Caleb barely noticed. He was warm on the inside, thanks to Kristen and her birthday party ideas.

Collar turned up against the wind, Caleb poured feed into a trough while Pops was inside the barn, bottle-feeding the orphaned calf.

Caleb hummed a silly song, one Kristen had assigned as his penalty for losing one of her games. He still couldn't believe how much fun he'd had playing those games and listening to Kristen laugh. She could be a bossy thing, forcing him and Pops to play kids' games he'd heard of but never played. Charades. Minute to Win It, which had consisted of tossing marshmallows into a cup while standing on a strip of duct tape six feet across the room. When his toe had crossed the line, mostly on purpose, Kristen had gleefully penalized him. It was like living the childhood he'd never had.

Funny how something so simple with the right person could make a man this happy.

He hung the bucket on the fence and headed inside the barn, out of the wind. He'd have a busy day, moving hay to various pastures, counting cows, checking heifers. The weatherman was predicting a winter storm this weekend. He might have to cancel his weekly meeting at the fitness center with the group of gangly, struggling boys he mentored for Child Services. He disliked canceling but if there was the slightest chance of a storm, he had to get the animals ready. The house, too. With Pops on dialysis, a power outage could spell disaster.

Pops came out of a stall, empty bottle in hand. The calf followed, nudging at him. Rip moved between man and animal to force the little one back inside.

"Somebody had a good time last night," Pops said.

Was he still humming? "Can't remember laughing that much in a while."

"It was good for you. Good for both of us."

For those hours, he'd forgotten Kristen's true reason for being at the ranch. He'd even forgotten how sick Pops was. "Hard to imagine you're all that sick, the way you were hopping around on one foot last night."

Pops gave Rip's head a rub. "Couldn't think of any other way to act out a flamingo. I sure ain't pink."

They both chuckled, remembering.

"She's a fine girl."

Caleb took off his gloves, slapped them against his thigh, not even pretending not to know who Pops meant. "Can't argue that."

"Pretty. Smart. A real Christian, the kind you don't find every day."

"What are you getting at, Pops? If you're matchmaking, save your breath."

"And what if I am? I may not be that old, but if things don't look up real soon, I won't be around this ranch forever."

Caleb clenched his hands. "Don't talk like that."

"Son, death is a fact of life for everyone. My ticket to heaven was paid in full by Jesus a long time ago. I'm not scared of dying, but I am scared of leaving you alone."

Emotion thickened in Caleb's throat. He couldn't have gotten a word out if he had to.

"See, it's like this, Caleb. When I adopted you, you thought I was helping you. Truth was, I was the one in need. I needed you."

"Aw, Pops." He stared at his boots, chest aching.

"I don't have a lot of regrets. I've lived most of my life the way I thought the Lord wanted me to. But I have one, a big one."

"What's that?"

"I regret not marrying and having the kind of family Kristen talks about. You missed out on that."

"So did you."

"Too late for me, but not for you. I want to see

you settled before I leave this planet. I want to dance a Cajun jig at your wedding, and if God wills, stick around long enough to hold my first grandchild."

"She's got a boyfriend."

"You sure about that? Couldn't tell it by the way she was laughing with you last night. Sparkly-eyed, she was, looking at you. And you're looking back."

"Kristen's nice to everyone."

"Keep telling yourself that, boy, and she'll marry somebody else before you get out of first gear. A woman like Kristen is special. She won't be left on the vine too long."

"You're shivering. Better get in the house."

Pops pinned him with a glare. "Changing the subject won't change the facts. You think about what I said. You don't want to be ten years down the road like I was, kicking yourself for being stubborn and stupid."

With that, Pops whirled and marched out of the barn, his frail body bent into the wind. Frigid air whipped in behind him. Caleb shivered, too. He'd never heard Pops talk like that and it scared him. He'd always thought Pops was happy with the bachelor life, and he'd figured if it was good enough for Greg Girard, it was good enough for Caleb.

Pops's admission got him thinking. About

Kristen. And kids. She'd be a fantastic mother. She'd read to her kids and rock them to sleep and throw wonderful birthday parties. Stuff he'd only fantasized about.

What would it be like to be part of that? To have his own family, his own kids, to have Kristen at his side forever?

He rubbed both hands over his face with enough vigor to cause a rash.

All the talk in the world didn't change the facts of who he was. No matter what Pops thought, Caleb didn't stand a chance with a woman like Kristen.

Chapter Five

Cold rain battering her uncovered head, Kristen darted from the doctor's office to the parking lot. Her run wasn't her usual 10K pace, but with the boot officially gone, she'd be back up to speed in a few weeks.

Inside the car, she wiggled her foot. It seemed like a lifetime since she'd been able to wear a real shoe. Even though the shoes were nursing clogs, they were way better than the heavy boot.

She couldn't wait to show Caleb. Greg, too, of course. And her family. They'd all be thrilled. Not just Caleb.

The fact that the cowboy was on her mind pretty much every waking moment gave her pause. They were spending a lot of time together. That was part of the reason. The other part was confusing. One moment, she thought he liked her. The next, he was backing away. She didn't want to play the rejection game again.

They'd had a grand time on Caleb's birthday, and the teasing had continued after another talk at the Oak Street Church two evenings ago. Underneath his reserve, Caleb was a great guy.

She started the car, cranked up the heat and the wipers. Slushy rain spit against her windshield. She frowned at it. Was that sleet? Or maybe snow? Tonight was Terri Bates's baby shower. As one of the planners, she hoped they didn't have to cancel. The cake was already made, the finger foods ordered and the guest list confirmed.

Her cell phone jingled. She fished it from her bag and answered.

"Hi, Mom."

"I'm just checking on you, sugar. The weather is supposed to get bad."

"I know, but I still have patients to see."

"How many?"

"Two who are essential. The others can be delayed or rescheduled if necessary. Right now, it's only slushy rain."

"Slushy rain brings freezing rain. The meteorologist is predicting a major ice storm. You know how dangerous that can be."

Oklahoma ice storms were terrifying. Last

year, six traffic fatalities occurred during a single-day event.

"Hopefully, the worst will hold off until after sundown when the temperature drops. By then, I'll be safely home." Making shower-cancelation calls to fifty people.

"Call or text when you get back to your apartment. You know I won't relax or stop praying until you do."

"Thanks, Mom. I appreciate the prayers, but don't worry. I lived in the mountains long enough to know how to drive in bad weather." Granted, Colorado mostly saw snow. No need to remind her mother of that.

"Remember the rules Dad taught you."

Kristen smiled, but dutifully ticked off her dad's ingrained instructions. "Drive slowly, especially on bridges and overpasses, and steer into a skid."

"Preferably stay off the roads altogether. But if you do find yourself in an ice storm, stay wherever you are until it's safe to drive or Dad comes to get you."

"Will do, Mom. Thanks. I love you." What would she do without her strong, supportive family?

"Be safe. I love you, too."

She rang off and headed to her first patient, wipers flapping with the rhythm of the radio.

The weather in Oklahoma was fickle. It might not do anything at all.

By the time she reached the Girard ranch, tension knotted Kristen's shoulders. She leaned close to the windshield, squinting through the heavy, pounding onslaught of slushy rain.

"So much for hoping this would blow over," she grumbled.

She prayed she'd be able to get Greg's treatment in and get home before the storm strengthened.

As she parked her Honda, the front door of Caleb's house opened and he stomped out. Head down, no coat, he jogged to the car and yanked the door open.

"Have you lost your mind?" He looked as dark and stormy as the skies.

Kristen stiffened. "What are you talking about?"

"Don't you watch the weather? Turn around and go home right now while you can."

"Your dad needs his treatment, as you well know." He was starting to make her mad. "And I'm not leaving until he gets it."

"That's stupid. Pops wouldn't want you to risk your life." Fat drops of rain pummeled his head. She was tempted to do the same.

"I'm already here. And you aren't well trained

enough to do the treatment by yourself." Hurt by his tone, she shoved her nursing bag into his gut and pushed past him to get out of the car. "Let's do this, so I can get out of your way."

She started up the rise, fueled by wounded annoyance and not caring if he remained out in the rain and cold until he turned into a Popsicle.

The silly notion cooled some of her anger. But she didn't wait for him. She marched up on the porch, pushed open the wooden door and went right in, closing it behind her.

Take that, cowboy.

Before she could unwind her scarf, Caleb entered, dripping wet and puffing like a steam engine. He glared at her. She glared back. What was his problem? Was he already sick of her?

The collie rose from his spot by the fireplace and came to greet her. She rubbed his ears, trying to decide what to say to Caleb.

"I'll get towels," he said. From his expression, he'd probably strangle her with them. He plunked her nurse's tote on a chair and left her alone with the dog.

"Grouch," she said. Rip wagged his tail and looked sweet.

From the back of the house, an area she hadn't seen, she heard male voices. One was quiet and soothing, the other hot and loud.

What was he so mad about?

She removed her coat and gloves, but they were wet, so she waited by the door. Rip waited with her, licking the moisture from her clogs.

Both Girard men entered the room together. Caleb didn't look quite so thunderous. He'd dried off and his boots were missing.

He hadn't even noticed that her boot was missing, too.

Pops took one look at her face and asked, "Did he bark at you?"

Kristen bent to pat the collie again. "No, he's a sweet dog. He likes me."

Pops snorted. "I meant Caleb."

"Oh." Her gaze flashed to the cowboy. "A little."

"Don't take it to heart. He fusses like an old hen because he's worried about you. Does me that way all the time."

"Pops." Caleb shook his head and handed her a towel. "Warm from the drier."

His tone was nicer.

"Thank you. This feels wonderful."

She patted her face and hair, wiped off her coat and dabbed at her scrubs. Rip had taken care of her shoes. Caleb reached for her coat and she gave it to him. He hung it on the back of a chair close to the fire. Was that his form of an apology?

"Beastly out there, huh?" Pops said. "You

want some coffee? You like cocoa better, don't you? Caleb, make her some cocoa."

"That's not necessary," she said. Caleb was grumpy enough. No use ordering him to make refreshments. He'd likely blow a fuse.

Naturally, the cowboy ignored her protest and went into the kitchen. She could see him from the open-concept living room, moving around, taking down the ingredients for hot chocolate. He opened the fridge. Took out milk. Clunked a pan against the metal burner.

Then, and only then, did he look at her, his expression unreadable. "Get going on Pops's treatment, so you can get out of here."

Okay. Fair enough. Like Pops said, he was concerned about the weather.

His motive might be good, but his delivery needed work.

"You need to be in on the instructions," she said.

Caleb shot her a frosty look and turned off the burner with a heavy sigh. She ushered Pops into the bedroom, where he relaxed in his recliner while they went through the protocol. Caleb kept looking from the machine to the window and back again. Maybe he was afraid of storms?

When the machine was set to run for the next few hours, she handed Greg the remote and put a stack of magazines at his elbow. "Need anything else?"

"If I do, I'll holler. Go on and have that cocoa."

Caleb went ahead of her to the kitchen. The ingredients were in the pot. All he had to do was turn on the stove.

Kristen leaned a hip against the counter and faced him. The kitchen was small, and they were close.

She could see the outline of his whiskers, which had darkened with the day. Masculine. Attractive. She swallowed, looked down and watched his competent, cowboy hands as he prepared the hot drink. He worked without much thought, a man accustomed to caring for himself.

A frisson of pity surprised her. Caleb had cared for himself basically all his life. No mama or daddy to guide him the way she'd had. No one to call and make sure he was safe in a storm. No one to come to his rescue or kiss his boo-boos or listen to his dreams. Yet behind the gruff exterior, he'd become a good, steady man, fiercely loyal to the one person who'd treated him well. And Mom claimed he spent his Saturday mornings with a group of troubled teens, the way Pops had done for him.

A chunk of her heart melted.

He handed her a cup of steaming chocolate. A

handful of mini marshmallows floated on top, the way she liked it.

She sipped, watching him over the top of her cup.

He sipped his, returning her stare.

Neither spoke for a long time.

Only the *click* of the dialysis monitors and Rip's gentle snore broke the silence. It was a surprisingly comfortable silence. Eye to eye, sipping at the sweet liquid in the warm, cozy kitchen while, outside, winter tormented the earth.

When she sipped and came up with a marshmallow mustache, Caleb lips tilted. He handed her a paper towel. "I owe you an apology."

"It's okay."

"Pops was right. I bark when I'm worried. It's getting nasty outside."

"The drive out here wasn't too bad."

"That's changing rapidly." He hitched his head toward the outdoors. "Look outside."

Kristen set her cup on the counter and went to the double windows in the living room. Caleb followed, standing close enough that his leather-and-woods scent circled around her, heady.

"Oh, no."

Sleet pounded the earth, already turning the yard white.

"That's not snow."

Snow, she could handle. "Do you think the roads are freezing over yet?"

"The ground was already frozen. Add freezing rain and then sleet and you're looking at roads of solid ice."

Tension sprang up in Kristen's shoulders. Driving home in the dark in an ice storm could spell disaster.

Caleb had one nerve cell left and it was sparking like a broken highline.

Having Kristen here in his house day after day was both glorious and awful. He was like a puppy, eager to see her but terrified of being kicked.

The woman had a boyfriend. But ever since his talk with Pops, Caleb kept imagining Kristen in a lacy wedding gown.

Now here she was in the flesh, and he kept having the same vision. Only the wedding wasn't for her and some rich doc. It was for him and her, followed rapidly by a breath-grabbing vision of her rocking his baby in a wooden rocker with a sweet Madonna smile on her lips.

He was going seriously nuts.

To add to his torment, curtains of sleet hammered his house and gave no sign of letting up.

To make one final check of the animals, he left the house, Rip at his side, while R2-D2 filtered Pops's blood. He slipped a few times, almost fell. Once he went down but managed to grab the shed door and pull himself back to his feet. He went inside the small shed to test-fire the generator. Just in case.

He started back to the house, shocked at how much the conditions had deteriorated since he'd first come outside. Ice pellets sluiced down the collar of his coat. Sleet stung his cheeks. He shivered, moving as fast as he could without taking another tumble.

They were in for a doozy of an ice storm. He had to get Kristen home. Fast.

By the time Greg's treatment was complete, the TV on the wall was warning motorists to stay off the roads.

"You need to get out of here," he told Kristen.

She frowned at the windows. "That bad?"

"Vicious."

He helped her gather her supplies, stewing, thinking. Was it safe for her to drive?

Greg had followed them into the living room. He stood at the front windows. "Looks too treacherous, Kristen. Maybe you ought to stay here until this settles down."

Caleb's heart slammed against his rib cage. *Yes. No!*

He wasn't the sort of man who encroached on another man's territory. Having Kristen under his roof any longer than it took to do the treatments would kill him…as in hammer him in the head dead. He'd implode like one of those buildings loaded with dynamite. Only the dynamite inside him was all the words he wanted to say, the love he wanted to share.

"I'll make it." Kristen wound the plaid scarf around her pretty neck. "It's not that far into town."

Four miles might as well be a thousand on wet ice.

"Maybe I should drive you."

She gave him one of those insulted, I-am-woman looks and exited the house.

With more misgivings than a debutante in a pigpen, Caleb watched from the porch. Sleet swirled up in his face, pitted his cheeks. His eyes burned from the cold.

She'd walked less than two yards when her vinyl clogs slipped. Her arms windmilled.

Bolting from the porch in one leap, he skidded behind her in time to stick out his arms, but not in time to brace his legs.

Kristen fell back against him. He circled her waist. His boots slipped.

They went down. *Hard.*

All he could feel was the frozen ground, Kristen's puffy coat and the freezing rain melting against his scalp.

He battled to a stand, somehow bringing her up with him. The ground was slicker than a used-car salesman. Any second, one of them could unbalance the other and down they'd go.

"Are you hurt?" He turned her to face him.

"No."

"What about your leg…" He looked down, suddenly realizing what was different about her today. "Your boot is gone."

She huffed. "Took you long enough to notice."

Was he *supposed* to notice?

Holding on to his arm, Kristen started toward her Civic again. They slipped, almost went down again.

She was starting to make him mad. Barking mad, as in worried. "It's idiotic to think you can drive in this."

She turned his arm loose and slid the rest of the way to the vehicle, slamming into the side. Holding on to the ice-covered car, she turned her head, glaring. "Are you calling me an idiot?"

Caleb's shoulders heaved. He slid in next to her, using the car as support. His breath puffed white fog. The freezing rain was giving him hypothermia.

"I didn't mean it that way. I just don't like the idea of you out by yourself in this kind of weather. If you wreck or run off in a ditch—"

"I have a cell phone."

Irritating, independent woman. "But no one will be able to get to you. Be sensible and let me drive you home."

"What makes you think you can drive any better than me?"

When had she become so unreasonable? "My truck is heavy, a three-quarter-ton four-wheel drive. We stand a better chance of actually getting to town in it than in your lightweight car."

She considered for less than a second. "My dad would agree with you."

"One sensible Andrews anyway," he grumbled. "I'll bring the truck around. Wait inside your car out of this weather."

He made his way up the rise to the carport. Driving in this weather was madness. But Kristen wanted to go home, and he wanted her safe and sound and out of his house. He yelled in the back door to let Pops know where he was going, got in his truck and drove carefully out to the road.

He waited while Kristen locked her car—as if some fool would be out burglarizing cars tonight—then slid her way to his truck, where she slammed into the side. Laughing. The crazy woman was laughing.

Nothing was funny to him right now.

He'd get out and open her door, but the truck

would probably slide off on its own. Not a happy thought.

Using the overhead handle, she pulled herself up and into the cab, taking care, he noted, to keep her weight off the formerly broken leg.

"If I wasn't trying to get home, the icy ground would be fun."

"You're not a rancher." He'd probably have three babies tonight, all of them in danger of freezing to death in this wet, cold weather unless he stayed out in the barn with the mamas. "Buckle up and hold on."

Once she was settled, he eased off the brake. Traction was limited, but the truck crawled forward.

They didn't talk. Tension filled the cab. Caleb thought his shoulder muscles might snap in half.

Kristen leaned forward, staring out at the crystallized terrain as if her kryptonite eyes could melt the ice. Caleb focused on holding the truck on the road. No one else had driven this way since Kristen had come in. No tracks, no ruts, and the dirt and gravel had disappeared beneath a thick sheet of ice. Nothing to give him traction.

They'd traveled less than a quarter mile when he started up a small hill. The truck slowed to a crawl. He gently pressed the accelerator. All four wheels spun. The truck slipped to one side.

Caleb eased off the gas pedal. And the truck began a slow, silent slide. Backward.

Caleb was helpless to stop it. One tap of the brakes and they'd be in a ditch or worse, upside down.

Holding the wheel, he did his best to stay on the road until gravity stopped them at the bottom of the hill.

Kristen looked at him with worried eyes. "I don't think we can do this, Caleb."

Suddenly, it hit Caleb like a brick to the face. The woman he couldn't get out of his head or his heart, the woman who belonged to a Colorado doctor, was stranded in the ice storm. Maybe for days. With him.

Chapter Six

Somehow, Caleb had managed to back the truck all the way to the ranch house. He'd been too tense to talk, but when he'd finally put the truck in Park, Kristen had exploded with conversation. She was grateful, admiring. For the moment, Caleb was her superhero.

He liked the feeling. Liked it a lot. Fool that he was. All he'd done was drive.

Now they were in the house, standing side by side, shoes and coats cast aside for the warmth of the fireplace. Kristen was next to him, making his head swell and his neck sweat. He thought he'd die if she didn't move, and he was sure he would if she did.

Yeah. He was one messed-up cowboy.

She stretched out her hands. "You were right."

He tilted his face toward her. "About?"

"How bad the storm was going to be."

"Rancher's intuition. I've felt this coming for a while." He offered an amused smile. "I also happened to watch the weather."

She bumped him with her shoulder. "Seriously. Intuition counts. Nurses are like that about full moons. More accidents. More babies."

"Tonight will be the same." He turned toward the kitchen. "I'll have to check the cows soon. Might as well rustle up some food now."

"Let me help."

"I've got it. You can…watch TV or read or something."

"I'd rather cook. But first, I need to cancel a baby shower I'm supposed to cohost tonight, and call my parents to let them know I'll be staying over."

Staying over. Caleb shivered. And he wasn't cold. Staying over meant she'd be here tomorrow. Maybe the next day.

He opened the freezer compartment and stared inside.

She was here. Might as well enjoy it. Pretend a girl like her could care about a guy like him. He could face reality later.

Cooking with Caleb, which sounded like a show on the Food Network, turned out to be much more fun than cooking alone, or even with Mom. And Kristen loved cooking with Mom.

More than once, she bumped into the trim cowboy, sometimes intentionally, sometimes not. He growled a few times, which made her laugh.

"All bark," she said, when he pointed a fork at her.

If she had to be stranded, the Girard ranch was a good place. Even though Caleb was sometimes as complicated as a book on nuclear physics, she loved being around him. He knew so many interesting things, about animals, nature, life, politics. And the gentle, sacrificial way he cared for his dad absolutely melted her. He was, she realized, looking after her, too. The thought made her feel safe, secure, no matter the storm outside.

With a slow dawning, she realized she still had a mountain of a crush on the handsome cowboy.

Together in his kitchen, they joked, jostled and talked until Greg picked up his laptop and said, "I'll work in the bedroom. Y'all are noisy."

She and Caleb exchanged an amused grimace.

"Keeping records isn't his favorite pastime." Caleb thwacked at a head of lettuce with a fierce-looking knife. The ranchers actually had fixings for salad, a real shocker. "Turns him into a grouch."

She tapped an egg against the counter and emptied it into a bowl. "Takes one to know one."

He laughed, a genuine, happy laugh that accented the tiny lines around his eyes. Something sweet settled over Kristen, sweeter still than the night of Caleb's birthday. She liked his laugh. Liked him, regardless of how confusing he could be.

When he'd caught her in his arms earlier, she'd experienced a powerful jolt of attraction.

Mulling that disconcertingly delightful moment, Kristen opened an overhead cabinet. Inside were a can of soup, two cans of tamales and a box of Jiffy corn bread mix.

"Where are your spices?"

The knife stopped thwacking. "Other than salt and pepper?"

"Please tell me you have oregano and garlic powder."

"What if I don't?"

"Then these meatballs will not be as wonderful as I'd planned." She dumped a half cup of bread crumbs into the bowl.

"Pops and I'll eat anything," Caleb said, "especially if someone else cooks it."

Kristen snorted. "I'm not sure that's a compliment."

"It wasn't?" he asked, and his innocent expression made her giggle.

"Do you or do you not have any other spices?"

He opened another cabinet and took out two

bottles, holding them up with a sheepish grin. "Would cinnamon or chili powder work?"

"Cinnamon meatballs and spaghetti?"

"Maybe not." He stuck the bottle back in the cabinet and offered the other. "Chili's good in anything."

She laughed. "Not in Chef Kristen's meatballs."

"Aw, come on, Chef." He leaned in close to the bowl as if he was going to sprinkle in the spice. "Take a chance. Try something new."

He was as close as a whisper, his eyes dancing, his leather-and-woods scent filling up her head. *Take a chance. Try something new.*

Or maybe *someone* new.

The thought caught her off guard, tangled in her head, twined around her heart.

Something sizzled in this kitchen. And it wasn't the food.

Much later, after the meal and cleanup, followed by a game of dominoes, which Greg easily won, the older cowboy retired to his bedroom and left them alone.

"He looks tired," Kristen said, after the door down the hall closed. "Didn't eat much, either. Was it my cooking?"

"No. The meatballs, even without your fancy spices, were terrific. Pops puts on a good front, but he's not been himself for a while now."

"Some dialysis patients do pretty well."

"Pops isn't one of them."

"Dialysis can drain a person, and that's not a pun. Their loved ones, too, only in a different way." Aching for him, Kristen put a hand on his shoulder. "I admire you, Caleb. You've been strong for him."

"I feel helpless."

"You're not. You've been proactive, not only taking on the load here, but by gaining prospective donors."

"None of which match."

"Yet. We have still have people in the process and another church group to speak to before Christmas."

"What if that's a bust, too?"

"Then we'll go to another town. Maybe Pecan Valley."

"Not there."

His harsh tone shocked her. "Why not?"

"I lived there before. A long time ago."

She understood. With her chest aching, she asked, "When you were a boy?"

He nodded. "Before my mother decided I was too much trouble to keep."

"Oh, Caleb. I'm sorry for all you've been through."

"Don't be. I'm sorry enough for myself. I'd like to forget and put it behind me, but it never stays there. Pops has been more than a dad to me. I couldn't have asked for better. But there's this spot inside—" He stopped as if he'd revealed too much.

The wounds of childhood ran deep. "Abandonment is an awful thing."

"Yeah," he said harshly. "She left me in a truck stop. Told me she'd be right back. That was the last time I ever saw her."

"How old were you?"

"Seven. And so mad at the world no foster family could stand me. If not for Pops—" His voice choked.

"Did you ever find out what happened to her? I mean, couldn't she have been in an accident or something?"

"'Or something' is about right. She left with a trucker. Police caught up to her a few months later. She refused to take me back."

Dear God, she prayed silently. *What do I say that could even come close to healing such a gaping, ugly, unforgettable wound?*

She rubbed the tension in his shoulder, a nursing move she'd done for patients many times. But with Caleb, the action felt personal. She let her hand drop. "It can't be easy to talk about."

"I usually don't. Don't know why I am now, but there's my baggage, opened for inspection." His tone was bitter. "Such a warm, loving family

I come from. But who could blame her? I was a horrible kid."

"Who became a strong and good man." She touched him again, this time not caring that it felt personal. He'd opened his heart to her. That was about as personal as a man could get. "You may have every reason to be bitter, Caleb, but you don't have to go on feeling that way. God can heal you on the inside, where it hurts so much."

Caleb didn't respond, and disappointment skittered through Kristen. If only Caleb understood how much peace there was in knowing Jesus.

Praying silently, Kristen crossed to the windows to look out. Darkness lay over the land. She flipped on the porch light. Ice covered the porch and sidewalk, and the visible patch of yard was white.

Caleb remained by the table where they'd played dominoes. A quiet tension stretched from him to her like an elastic cord.

He shifted, cleared his throat. "You'll be okay while I go out and check on a couple of cows?"

"Sure." She understood. He'd revealed too much and he was embarrassed. "Text if you need help."

His mouth softened. "You know anything about birthing cows?"

"I know about birthing humans."

"Too cold. Stay here, stay warm." He started to move.

"Caleb."

He stopped, looking at her in question.

"I'm not sorry you told me. Don't you be sorry, either. You aren't responsible for your childhood."

His Adam's apple bobbed. He nodded, then clicked his tongue at the dog. Rip rose, stretched his front legs out in front of him, gave an all-over shake and trotted toward the back door with his master.

Kristen clicked on the TV, watched the Weather Channel long enough to know she'd be stranded for a while and then discovered a favorite old movie was about to begin. Taking the flannel throw from the back of the couch, she curled her sock feet beneath her and settled in.

By the time Caleb stomped back in the house, toting an armload of firewood, the movie had started and she was once again rooting for Sandra Bullock's character to fall for the nice guy.

She hopped up from the couch. "Let me help."

"I got it." He dumped the load of wood into a container at the end of the fireplace. "Rip could use a towel, though."

So could his owner.

"Tell me where they are."

"Laundry room." He jerked his chin toward the back of the house.

She found the laundry room off the kitchen near the back entry and loaded the towels into a basket.

As she entered the living room again, she asked, "Any baby calves?"

She set the basket on the bar dividing the living room and kitchen, took out two towels and handed one to Caleb.

"One. Safe and warm in a stall. The other pregnant heifers are in the pasture closest to the barn."

"Will you have to watch them all night?"

"Every few hours." He shed his jacket and ran the towel over damp brown hair. "You'd think they'd want to go in the barn, but they don't."

She took his coat, feeling domestic and wifely as if Caleb was hers and she belonged here with him. The thought ratcheted her pulse.

The heavy duck material was covered in melting ice pellets and smelled cold and masculine. After hanging it on a chair back near the fireplace to dry out, she crouched in front of Rip and gave him a brisk rubdown.

"His ears are cold," she said.

Caleb added a log to the fire and stirred it. Sparks crackled, joining the ones inside her.

"Yours would be, too."

"I'd wear a hat."

"He won't. I asked him. He says it's sissy." Caleb's smile lines crinkled.

A light, airy feeling bubbled up in Kristen's chest. She loved the teasing side of Caleb.

"Would you like some coffee? I made a pot while you were out." Another wifely action that made her imagination crazy.

She'd never felt this way with anyone else.

Was the teenage crush becoming something more? Or was it only the close quarters that made her feel this undeniable sense of rightness, as if she belonged here? With Caleb.

"Thanks. It'll be a long night."

"I'm sorry," she said.

"For?"

"The storm, the baby calves that might freeze if you're not out there, the imposition of being stuck with me." Was she hinting?

"You're not an imposition, Kristen. You could never be."

Something in the intensity of his voice sent shivers down her spine. She loved the sound of his voice, the rich baritone, the soft-spoken way he formed his words.

It must be a combination of the storm, their close proximity, the warm fireplace, but she was having a hard time remembering why she'd ever wanted to be with James Dudley.

"This is my favorite old movie," she said to break the sudden thickness in the atmosphere. "*While You Were Sleeping.* Ever seen it?"

He shook his head. "Don't think so."

"Well, cowboy, you have missed out. Got any popcorn?"

One side of his mouth kicked up. "You're going to force me to watch a chick flick *and* eat my popcorn?"

"I have it recording on DVR. We can start at the beginning if you'd like. It's only been on for about ten minutes. It's the sweetest, cutest movie."

He clutched his chest and pretended to stagger. "I'm not sure I can endure the pain of the whole thing."

Kristen wrinkled her nose at him. "You will love it. I promise."

He rolled his eyes, but led them into the kitchen to pop some corn.

Rip padded in behind them, nose tilted upward. When the popcorn stopped popping, Caleb dumped it into a bowl and tossed one fluffy bit into the air. Ripley caught it and thumped his hairy tail in thanks.

Kristen patted his ears. "Aren't you talented?"

"Just like his master" came Caleb's droll reply.

Kristen snickered. "You catch popcorn with your mouth, too?"

"Yep. See?" He tossed a kernel into his mouth.

"Let me see that popcorn." She pointed toward the couch. "Sit."

Both man and dog obeyed. She giggled. Caleb laughed. Even as a teenager, Caleb had been gorgeous when he laughed.

"You should do that more often," she said, plunking down beside him on the couch.

He snatched a handful of corn. "Do what? Sit on command, like my dog?"

"Laugh. Have fun. Be silly." He carried a heavy weight these days. "Play releases stress. And I know you have plenty of that, especially with Greg's illness."

"Yeah." He pointed at the TV. "What's about to happen?"

Message sent and received. He didn't want to talk about his stressors. She got it. She didn't want to talk about hers, either. She wanted to relax in this cozy room, stuff her face with salty popcorn and watch a movie. With Caleb.

"Lucy has a secret crush on Peter," she said, "the unconscious guy in the hospital bed, even though they don't actually know each other. A nurse mistakes her for Peter's fiancée and tells his family, who embrace her. They're so excited that Peter found a nice girl that Lucy doesn't want to hurt them with the truth. Besides, Peter is in a coma. Meanwhile, Peter's brother, Jack, falls in love with Lucy, but no way is he going to mess with his brother's girl."

Caleb blinked at her in wide-eyed bewilderment. "Does that even make sense to you?"

She bumped his elbow with hers. "Oh, have some popcorn and watch. You'll see."

She clicked Play on the remote and started the classic romantic comedy. Caleb reached for another handful of popcorn and settled in close to her. She hadn't expected that, but she didn't mind. Not one tiny bit. Caleb made funny, caustic remarks, groaned in a spot or two, but soon was chuckling at the comedy. When a tender, romantic scene flashed on the screen, he grew quiet.

With Lucy and Jack falling into a near kiss, Kristen's breath shortened. Her arms tingled. A pulse began to beat in her throat. The movie had never affected her that way before. Was it Caleb's closeness?

All he had to do was shift his arm and it would be around her shoulders. To her shock, she wanted that very much. As reserved as he was, Caleb would probably never make the first move, but Kristen had the sudden urge to rest her head against his chest, listen to his strong heartbeat and watch two movie characters fall in love.

The atmosphere thickened in the quiet room.

Was he feeling it, too? And what if he was? Did it mean anything? Did she want it to?

"By now," she said to break the strange mood, "I'm rooting for Jack and wishing he would speak up and tell Lucy that he loves her."

"But what about Lucy's feelings? She's in love with Peter."

"She only thinks she is. She'll come to her senses."

Caleb gave her the strangest look. "Only in the movies."

What was that supposed to mean? And why did it make her sad?

They grew quiet while Lucy was swept up in preparations for her wedding to Peter.

When Jack walked away from Lucy without admitting his love, Kristen said, "I've seen this a dozen times and I'm still getting teary. Why doesn't he *say something*?"

"Just because a man loves a woman doesn't mean he's right for her."

"But he is. And it's such exquisite torture waiting for them both to figure it out."

"Exquisite torture." He gave her a long, searching look. "That's about the sum of it."

Chapter Seven

Caleb woke at seven the next morning, late for him, but considering his frequent night treks to look in on the cows, he hadn't slept much. He had, however, had plenty of time to think. Mostly about Kristen.

Watching a romantic movie with her close enough that he could smell her coconut scent had, indeed, been exquisite torture. He'd loved it. He'd hated it. Because like Jack in the movie, he was in love with someone else's woman. Only this was real life, not a movie with a guaranteed happy ending.

That was what scared him so much with Pops. They weren't guaranteed anything, much less a happy ending.

After he'd dressed and gone outside to check on the new arrivals, he returned for breakfast. The seductive scent of bacon pulled him into the kitchen. Pops sat at the bar, sipping a tiny glass of cranberry juice.

Pops lifted a hand. "'Morning."

"'Morning." Caleb gave a brief nod and headed for the coffeepot.

"This is the day the Lord has made. Rejoice in it, son," Pops said, as he did every single morning. "How is it out there?"

Caleb wondered how a dying man could find joy in watching his days fly past. "Not too bad. Wind died down. Snowed about three inches."

"It snowed?" A spatula clattered against the stove as Kristen whipped around.

"Still falling. Nice, dry snow, too."

"I can drive in snow."

"Not with two inches of ice under it."

"Oh." She looked disappointed, and he felt a stab of unexpected grief that she wanted to leave. It was a dumb thing, but there it was.

"You didn't have to cook breakfast."

She turned back to the stove. "Paying for my restful night in your guest room. Pops says you like your eggs over easy. How many?"

"Two. Smells good in here."

"Biscuits in the oven."

"Real biscuits?" He and Pops usually just twisted open a can and stuck them in the oven.

"Yes, except you didn't have buttermilk so I had to improvise."

"I didn't know a modern woman could bake real biscuits."

"Untrue stereotype. Today's woman simply has the choice to live her life the way she wants, and for me that includes baking."

Pops, who hadn't said much, chose that moment to crack. "A woman like that is a catch, son. Brings home the bacon and knows how to fry it up."

Kristen grinned at the older cowboy. "Spoken like a true chauvinist."

"No, ma'am. I just appreciate a good thing when I meet her. A man is only a man, but a woman is a gift from the Lord. And, boy, am I glad He decided to make good use of one of old Adam's ribs."

This time she laughed, her gaze gliding toward Caleb. "Your Pops is feisty this morning."

"You should be here when he's feeling good."

She cracked an egg against the edge of the pan. "You have dark circles. Used tea bags can help with that."

He snorted. "Life of a rancher. I'll catch up tonight." He crossed to the stove, snitched a piece of bacon. "We had three babies so far."

"There could be more?"

"Shouldn't be, but with the storm, I can't be sure. I'll ride out after breakfast and have a look."

He reached for the bacon plate and set it on

the table. Kristen had already put out plates, the utensils neatly lined on napkins, glasses in their proper places above the plates, saucers with knives across them. He had no idea what to do with that. It was a fancy table and another reminder of why he had no business in Kristen's life.

"I had a dream last night," Pops said as he moved from the bar to the table. "Got me wanting a Christmas tree."

Caleb gave him a look. "Must have been quite a dream."

Pops shook a napkin onto his lap the way the two of them never did when they were alone.

"I was a boy again, on the family home place. It was Christmas, and my brother and me were decorating a big old tree, talking about the wagon we wanted from Santa." He shook his head, gazing down at the plate in nostalgia. "It was the best feeling. Best I've had a long time."

Kristen set the plate of eggs on the table. "Family dreams like that are so lovely."

He wouldn't know. He'd never had any. Not good ones anyway.

"So I got to thinking." Pops slid two eggs onto his plate. "Let's put up a tree this year."

Caleb took the biscuits from Kristen and set them on the table. Then he held the chair while she sat. "We never put up a tree."

"No law says we can't."

"That's a wonderful idea, Greg," Kristen said, all smiles and sparkles so that Caleb wanted to give her the world.

"After breakfast, you and Caleb can go and cut one. There are plenty down in the woods."

"I got cows to look after."

"You can check the cows while you're out looking for my tree."

Caleb knew arguing was useless, and he didn't want to refuse Greg anything. Kristen, either, if he was honest. "I can get it. Kristen doesn't need to get out in the cold."

"But I want to. I love snow. Remember? Colorado?"

Yeah. He remembered. How could he forget? Colorado was where the good doctor lived.

"Whatever you want." He shoved a biscuit into his mouth to keep from saying more.

This might be Pops's last Christmas. If the only person who'd ever given a flying cow chip about him wanted a tree and wanted Kristen to go along, Caleb would do it. Even if it was "exquisite torture."

They walked out into a pretty snowfall, plump flakes swirling in lazy circles, as white and lacy as a wedding dress. Caleb didn't want to think about wedding dresses. Pops may have dreamed of Christmas trees, but Caleb had dreamed of white lace and an auburn-haired woman with a sunny disposition and ready smile.

It was a killer dream, brought on, he was sure, by the fact that Kristen was under his roof. Now the lacy snow was a reminder he didn't need that he was crazier about her today than he'd ever been.

Why couldn't he have fallen in love with someone attainable?

Ripley flushed birds from an overhead oak, rattling the snow loose. It drifted down around them, a feathery fairyland. Made a man feel almost poetic.

Kristen held out a glove and caught a flake. "Every snowflake is different. I guess you know that, but isn't snow the most incredible thing?"

Yeah, it was. Being an outdoorsman, he spent a lot of time pondering the wonders of nature. Snowflakes ranked right up there with the number of stars in the vast cosmos. And he was amazed that he knew a word like *cosmos.*

"How do you know they're all different?" he asked just to tease her. "Have you examined every single snowflake on the planet?"

"Smarty." She scooped up a handful of the soft snow and tossed it at him.

He ducked. "Missed me."

"Just wait." She shot him her mean look,

which caused a happy bubble in his chest. Kristen didn't have a mean bone in her body.

"Look at this landscape," she said. "I feel kind of bad walking in it."

She took another step and gazed down at her oversize footprints. She looked adorable in his too-big boots. Three pairs of his thick socks had made them fit, but nothing could make them graceful. "The snow is so pristine and perfect, like a vast white carpet of sparkling diamonds."

"I think that, too, sometimes." Though not quite as poetically. Fragile and fleeting, that was what Oklahoma snow was. Like this time with her.

She patted her gloved hands together in a cold gesture. "How far are the Christmas trees?"

She should have stayed at the warm house. He was accustomed to working outside in harsh conditions. She wasn't. "On the other side of this pasture along the fence line. If you're too cold we can go back. I'll saddle up and return later."

She shook her head, auburn hair swishing from beneath her bright blue cap. "I like cold weather. No way am I going to miss out on finding the perfect Christmas tree for your dad."

They tromped along with Rip darting in and out as if he was moving cattle. When a red cardinal flashed above the white ground, Caleb pointed. Kristen put a gloved hand against her heart and watched until the bird disappeared from sight.

She started talking about birds and nature, skiing and Colorado and how much she loved the mountains, but Oklahoma was home and she was so happy to be here, doing what she loved.

Caleb let the words flow around him and into him. The melody of her voice brought him pleasure, relaxed him, made him love her more.

He should have done a better job of guarding his feelings. But she'd owned his heart since the first time she'd cornered him at the burger joint, talking until he'd been relaxed enough and brave enough to kiss her in a dark movie theater.

It was a teenage first kiss, one of those momentarily awkward things that quickly blossomed into the sweetest, spiciest kiss of his life. Others came and had been forgotten, but not that one.

By the time they reached the evergreens, he barely noticed the cold. Kristen's cheeks were rosy, her breath a vapor and coming in puffs as she told him about her newest ideas for finding Pops a donor and then segued right into her plans for Christmas, and didn't he want to come to the Christmas program at church? Caleb didn't respond to that any more than he had the other snatches of conversation, but he'd heard her and remembered how important her faith was to her.

He wished he could believe that God cared. He wanted to, if only for Pops, who'd done his best to show Caleb the importance of a faith-filled life. Somehow the faith gene had missed him or, considering his worthless biological parents, had never been there to start with.

Kristen spotted the evergreens, gave a delighted little squeal and took off in a clumsy run.

"These are glorious," she called, reaching the stand of bushy green trees before he did. "Look at the snow on their boughs."

She was glorious, so heart-stoppingly pretty against the evergreens and the white landscape. So optimistic and joyous. Was it faith that caused her joy?

Caleb caught up with her, followed her around one crisp-scented tree and then another as they discussed and measured. He didn't really care as long as she kept talking in her animated voice, her eyes aglow, her cheeks pink. He loved seeing her happy. And her cheerful chatter, her sweet optimism filled some empty spot inside him.

"What about this one?" She stepped back away from a fluffy cypress, arms wide as if she might embrace the sticky limbs. He wanted to walk right into that embrace and never turn loose. "I'm envisioning this in front of those double windows, next to the fireplace."

"Sounds good to me." Dropping the ax, Caleb

started around to the other side in search of gaps. His boots found a slick patch of ice. His legs flew out from under him. He hit the soft snow with a shocked grunt.

Kristen hustled to his side, laughing, blue gloves to her lips. "Are you all right?"

"I'll live." He reached up. "Give a cowboy a hand?"

She fell for it…and yelped when he yanked her down. It was an ornery thing to do, but Kristen made him feel playful.

"You sneak!" Her gloved fists pummeled the front of his thick coat, causing him exactly no pain, but he did laugh. She was laughing, too, so that he knew she hadn't really minded the tumble. She rolled to one side, flapped her arms and legs and created an impromptu snow angel.

"You do it," she said.

And he thought, *Why not?* He'd never made a snow angel in his life, so he did. Snow flew around them like a white dust devil.

It felt remarkably good to cut loose this way, to let his bucket load of tensions flow out into the soft snow, to play like the kid he'd never been, to listen to the woman he loved laugh and talk. He could listen to her 24/7 and never grow tired of the soothing sound.

Arms and legs flung wide, he turned his

face to look at her. "We're destroying your perfect snow."

Her bright blue cap and gloves stood out like beacons against the white earth.

"It's okay. God made extra." She flapped her arms and sent snow flying. "Knowing Oklahoma, this will all be gone tomorrow. Might as well enjoy it. Want to go sledding later?"

He rolled his eyes. "Do I look like a man with a sled?"

"We don't need a sled. Trash can lids, cardboard boxes, old Slip 'N Slides."

"Oh, yeah, I have several old Slip 'N Slides lying around. The baby calves love playing on them in the summer."

Her eyes widened. She rolled forward to sit up, coat dusted with snow. "Seriously?"

"No." He found his footing and stood, snow drifting from his clothes, as he pulled her up with him. In the clumsy boots, she lurched forward, fell against him. Her slender arms went around his neck. She lifted her laughing face to his.

She sparkled, she glowed, and Caleb forgot the reasons he was wrong for her.

When she cupped his face with her fluffy blue gloves and kissed him, a soft brush of cold lips that ended too soon, Caleb's brain fogged. He couldn't let go. And she didn't try to move. Her green gaze bore into him as if she could reach inside his soul and see all the love he was terrified to give away. Maybe she knew, maybe she understood. She had the power to soothe him, to make him laugh, to get him up in front of a crowd to talk when he'd rather stick cacti in his eyes.

"Woman power," he whispered, right before he warmed her mouth with his. In some distant section of his brain, Caleb knew kissing Kristen Andrews registered on the Richter scale of dumbest things he'd ever done. She didn't love him, couldn't, and he had no business expecting her to.

But he ignored all that. It had been so long since he'd lost himself in a woman's kiss, *her* kiss, because that was the only one that had ever mattered. He wanted to relish the wonder of this one unexpected gift.

When Kristen melted against him like a snowflake, Caleb lost every mental argument along with most of his brain cells.

Kristen absorbed Caleb's body heat and the strength of his powerful arms holding her, caressing her back, massaging the soft, tickly place at the nape of her neck. The kiss was warm and sweet with a hint of spice, but reverent, too, the kind of kiss that felt like more than the simple joining of lips. This one came from somewhere deep in his heart to speak to hers.

And she was listening. *Oh, my.* Was she ever listening.

With a mood-breaking bark, Rip plowed into their legs, scattering snow, and forced them apart. In the clumsy boots, Kristen stumbled again. Caleb caught her, shushed the dog, then steadied her on her feet. She took one step back, putting a little distance between herself and the temptation of his embrace. She needed time to think and to sort the emotions rocketing through her as fast and powerful as a Cape Canaveral launch.

The truth was as obvious as the cold in her toes. She was falling in love with the hometown cowboy. Falling harder and faster and deeper than she had as a teenager. This was different. This was real and very possibly lasting.

Joy shot through her, a crossbow that pierced her heart and opened up the way for love. Love for Caleb Girard.

Oh. My. Word.

She stood up on her tiptoes and touched her lips to Caleb's again. "Much better than the last time we kissed."

Caleb tilted his head, looking at her with a mix of worry and happiness. "You remember the last time?"

"Down to the day and year." She rattled it off.

"Yeah," he said. "That was it."

"You remembered, too?"

"First kisses are unforgettable."

Was that all it had been? Memorable because it was his first kiss? Or could the seed of love have been planted that long-ago day in a small-town movie theater, and had their recent time together had made it grow?

He was a man now, not a teenager who didn't know how to deal with a woman who practically threw herself at him. Which was exactly what she'd done both then and now.

All those years ago, he'd simply walked away and ignored her. Would he do the same this time?

"Best Christmas tree hunt I've ever been on." He held her gaze with his.

"Except for Ripley, the intruding border collie." Her tone was wry.

The dog, clueless to sarcasm, heard his name and lifted a paw.

Caleb shook with one hand and patted the noble head with the other, but his gaze remained on Kristen. "As much as I like you, Rip, your timing really stinks."

And that admission made Kristen inordinately happy.

Decorating a Christmas tree proved every bit as enjoyable as he'd imagined. More so because he and Pops didn't own a single decoration, and they had to improvise. Better yet, because Kristen made his blood warm and his heart smile by chattering all the way back to the ranch. She'd held his hand—the one that wasn't leading the horse he'd commandeered to carry the tree. Her warmth had come through their gloves and captivated him. *She* captivated him.

Was he crazy? Was he about to get his heart stomped beyond repair? A woman like Kristen would never choose him over a rich, suave surgeon. She was too amazing, too smart and successful, too…good, for lack of a better word.

Today, he didn't care. Today, Kristen was in his house, and she'd kissed him like she meant it. He still couldn't wrap his head around that.

He'd never believed a man could live on hope. Today he believed.

He was feeling loose and hopeful, as if his tensions and worries and misgivings had blown away on the north wind.

"String or ribbon if you have it," Kristen was saying as she ticked off items on her fingertips while he secured the tree on a crossed-board stand. "Aluminum foil, spoons, old keys, any odds and ends you have lying around."

"I got plenty of rope," Caleb said.

She beamed. "Perfect! We'll use it as garland."

She wasn't put off by their lack of appropriate

decorations. With her usual energetic enthusiasm, she'd come up with the idea of decorating with found items.

"Plenty of junk around here." Greg smiled from Caleb to Kristen as if he suspected the reason for Kristen's rosy cheeks and Caleb's long glances. "Caleb, get our tackle boxes."

Caleb did as he was told, and they found a treasure trove of ridiculous items to hook or tie onto the tree limbs, everything from red-and-white bobbers to silver fish-shaped lures. Kristen proclaimed them perfect as she padded around the tree, still wearing his thick socks.

He thought she was the cutest thing, and when Greg wandered off somewhere for a minute, Caleb ducked behind their fun-filled tree with a stem of mistletoe he'd cut in the woods and held it over Kristen's head. She stood on her tiptoes and obliged, smiling against his mouth.

"How about a hat?" Greg's voice had them jumping apart.

Kristen snickered. "Between your dog and your dad…"

"Gotta get rid of those two," Caleb whispered to make her snicker again. Then, while she blushed and rearranged a feathered fishing lure, he went to see what Pops was yapping about.

Greg held up his best gray Stetson. "Don't

have a star or an angel, but how about this for the top?"

Kristen popped out from behind the tree and cried, "I love it!"

She had serious hat hair, little sprigs wiggling in the heated air from static electricity. Cypress needles stuck to the oversize sweatshirt Pops had loaned her.

He was about to tease her when her cell phone pinged.

The device rested on the hearth, where she'd set it after a call from her mother. Always hopeful for a donor call, Caleb reached for it to give to her. A name and face flashed across the lit screen.

James Dudley. The surgeon.

Chapter Eight

Kristen had never seen a man change so fast. Caleb had gone from teasing and romantic to solemn and silent in the time it took to take her phone from his outstretched hand.

What in the world?

She glanced at the screen. Shock ricocheted through her. James? Seriously? After he hadn't returned a single call or text, even the voice mail in which she'd wished him well and said it was time for them both to move on?

"You can read that. I'll give you some space." Caleb, who was inches away, watched her with a strange expression.

"Not necessary." She slid the phone into her pocket.

"If you were my girl, I'd expect a reply."

So he'd seen the caller ID. That explained the

sudden chill in the air. "I'm not his girl, Caleb. James and I are no longer together."

James had been nothing but a fantasy of the ideal man with plenty of money and a prestigious position in the community. And to him, she'd been nothing but another trophy for his shelf.

"Are you sure?"

"Do you think I'd be kissing you if I wasn't?"

"Don't know. Some girls would."

"Then you don't know me very well." She gave him a little chest push. "And, for your information, I'm not just *some* girl who goes around kissing any available guy."

He raked a hand over his head. His hair stuck up on top. Kristen resisted the urge to smooth it down. Instead, she glared at him for a long moment, hoping to burn her feelings into his thick head.

"You're right," he said softly. "You're not just any girl. You're special. You always have been. But I'm too lousy at relationships to even hope—" He stopped abruptly, turned away, shoulders stiff.

Kristen waited three beats, considering what to say. She didn't want to fight with him, not after their wonderful day. She knew about some of his wounds, but probably not all of them. His childhood had been anything but happy, and she had studied enough psychology in nursing school to understand the long-term effects of childhood trauma, especially abandonment.

She wouldn't fight. He didn't need that. She knew, without a doubt, that God's love could do what medical science couldn't. He could take the worst brokenness and make something beautiful from it.

From her peripheral vision, she saw Greg fade quietly from the room. She heard his door snick closed. In his wisdom, Greg was giving them the space to talk things out. She wouldn't be at all surprised if he was back there praying.

"Caleb," she said gently, stepping around in front of him. "Today has been… I don't even know how to describe how much I've loved today."

She reached for both of his hands. They were tough and masculine and heated from the fireplace.

He gripped her fingers as if they were his lifeline. "I loved it, too. Never wanted it to end."

Those were hard admissions for him to make. She could see that. And he'd said she was special as if he'd meant it.

"This is the first time I've even heard from James since moving back to Refuge. Those aren't the actions of a man in love. Forget him."

"Can you?"

"I already have." She kissed the top of his

rough cowboy hands. "Do you want to know about James and me? About what happened that finally opened my eyes to the kind of man he really is?"

"If you want to tell me."

She pointed. "Then sit down on that couch and listen to my pathetic little tale."

Caleb obliged. He knew he'd overacted to the phone call. It was her business. But one look at the face of the man a woman like her should marry, and he'd freaked out. The doc was a handsome guy, suave and rich looking, as if he had his hair cut in a salon where they served sparkling water in skinny little flutes and charged a hundred bucks a snip.

"James Franklin Dudley III," she said. "We met at the hospital where we both worked. All the nurses thought he was the hottest thing since incineration."

"I'm feeling better already," he said sarcastically.

"Hush. I'm not finished." She folded her feet under and turned toward him on the couch. "He was handsome, brilliant, witty—"

"And loaded?"

"Yes, but that wasn't the most important thing. We started dating. The usual stuff, dinner, dancing, fancy parties. He sent flowers and candy. Very attentive and flattering."

Oh, yeah, she was making him feel great. *He* loved her, and all he'd done was cut down a Christmas tree and ask her to decorate it with junk. And let her cook for him. The thought of flowers never crossed his mind. Some Romeo he was.

"I thought I was in love with him and I thought James felt the same. To be honest, I was too flattered to think straight. If I had, I would have known we were wrong together. When he invited me to join him on a ski trip to Vail, I was thrilled."

He hated this story.

"Anyway," she went on, "we had a great time the first day. Skied for hours, had a gorgeous dinner and then sat by the fire with cocoa, watching the snow fall on the mountains. It was dreamy."

He thought he might be sick. If there was a sad, ugly part to this tale, he wasn't seeing it.

"Then we went to our separate rooms, something I'd made clear from the start."

That made him feel a little better. He might live through this after all.

"Five minutes later, he tapped on the door. I let him in, of course, and then…" She sucked in a long breath, lost some of her exuberance.

"He wanted to stay. I said no, and we had a big argument. James said some rather ugly things, and then he stomped back to his room. I cried half the night."

"He made you cry?" Caleb's face was thunder.

"Yes, but I still didn't get what God was trying to show me. Sometimes I'm hardheaded like that." Her grin was sad. "The next morning, I went out to the slopes alone to think and pray. James knew my values, and I hoped that he'd simply been caught up in the moment and would behave differently after he'd slept on it."

"And?"

"I was lost in thought, not paying enough attention to my skis, and I fell."

"And broke your leg."

"The fibula, not a horrible bone to break as fractures go. I telephoned James and he rushed to the rescue like a white knight. He arranged the emergency rescue and went with me to the hospital."

"Did he apologize?"

"We didn't talk about it. I was in pain, remember? But when we got back to the ski lodge, he checked out and left. He didn't even tell me. In fact, he hadn't said a dozen nonmedical words to me through the entire ordeal. It was then I realized he was still very angry. Frankly, so was I. Angry and hurt. Even though I've called him, finally leaving a message that was better delivered in person, he hasn't responded. Not once. Until today."

"I see." He really didn't like this guy.

"So." She bounced one of his hands in hers. "Can we erase the last ten minutes and pick up where we left off? You and me, decorating the craziest tree in Christmasdom. Sneaking kisses under that withering bit of mistletoe."

"You sure?" His tone was almost wistful.

"I care about you, Caleb. Is that so hard to believe?" And was she crazy for tossing her feelings out there again for him to reject?

He touched her cheek. "I care about you, too."

She leaned into his hand. "Did you know I had a huge crush on you when we were teenagers? And did you know I orchestrated that impromptu date we had to the Rialto Theater?"

"You did?" When she nodded, he asked, "What about that smokin' kiss?"

"I think you started that. You did the shoulder slide maneuver." She demonstrated. "Next thing I knew we were all snuggled up watching some sci-fi show I said I was desperate to see."

The twinkle had returned to his eyes. "But you weren't?"

"I was desperate, but only for you to notice me." She handed him a fishing lure and pointed at a blank spot on the tree.

He hung the lure where she indicated. "I was noticing."

The old hurt throbbed, like her leg still did at times, so she asked the question that had haunted her for years. "Then why the cold shoulder later?"

And will it happen again when the ice storm is over?

"Besides the fact that your brothers were two of my best friends and they wouldn't like seeing their baby sister with the town troublemaker?"

"You weren't that bad. And you certainly aren't now."

"Thanks to Pops. He was tough on me, but tough because he cared. So I cleaned up my act."

No other man had ever paid enough attention to the wounded teenager to see his good qualities. Greg had.

Casually, she asked, "You know what would please him most?"

His hands stilled in adding yet another lure. "Yes. I know."

"Faith is important to me, too, Caleb. Greg and I want you to share it because we care about you."

He didn't reply and she thought perhaps she'd lost him again, but she was nothing if not persistent. She would not let him slip back into that silent shell of his.

"Christmas Eve service at our church is lovely. Maybe you could come. For me. For Greg." *For yourself,* she thought, but didn't say it.

He looked at her and something soft shifted through his features. "Maybe I will."

And Kristen decided to be satisfied with that.

When the ice and snow finally relented and Kristen returned home, the busy week of Christmas swarmed her. So much catch-up to do, though she had no regrets about the two days snowbound on the Girard ranch. Besides the fun they'd had gliding over the fields on plastic feed barrel lids, riding horses in the snow and building a Snoopy snowdog for Rip, she and Caleb had gotten to know each other as adults. He was, as she'd always suspected, a smart, complex, deeply caring man who held his emotions close to the vest. Watching him with Greg, with the baby calves, the dog and his apple-spoiled horse told her so much about him.

They'd given another talk where Kristen had shared her faith, her heart, and her belief that organ donation pleased the Heavenly Father. Every attendee, except those with serious health issues, took a card. She'd sniffled all the way home. Caleb had been ecstatic. He finally believed they had a chance.

It was a good start to Christmas week, and she

felt a sense of joy that had been lacking in her life for a while. Her social life was busy, but not until she and Caleb began seeing each had she realized how empty she'd been inside.

He filled her heart in a way no other man had. With James she'd always felt on edge as if she had to please him or lose him. With Caleb, she felt as if her heart had finally found a resting place, and that made Christmas all the more wonderful.

On Christmas Eve, after a long day of nursing visits, she stopped by Mom's before heading home to dress for church.

"Last load of gifts," she said, entering the house and crossing to the tree. Mom's tree was beautiful and elegant, but the funny tree at Caleb's ranch was her favorite.

"You spoil us." Mom's hair appeared freshly colored and styled. And she'd already dressed in a long red skirt and white blouse.

"You look gorgeous."

"Thank you, sugar." Her mother bent to arrange the gifts. She liked the packages organized just so.

"I think Caleb may come to church tonight."

"That's wonderful," Mom said. "Greg will be delighted."

"I'm delighted, too, Mom."

"Oh?" Mom straightened.

"I think I'm in love with him."

A tiny frown pulled at her mother's well-groomed eyebrows. "What about James? It's Christmas. Surely the two of you have mended differences by now."

"We haven't, and we won't. I broke it off, Mom. He texted a few days ago, a long time after my call, but I didn't reply."

"James is a successful physician with a huge future in front of him. And he's also of our faith. Shouldn't you give him a second chance?"

Yes, James attended church. Occasionally. But his behavior, which she would not share with her mother, didn't align with the scriptures he professed to believe in. "What matters is love and respect. James lost mine."

"At least call the man one more time and wish him a merry Christmas. Maybe he wants to apologize."

It was only a phone call. And it was Christmas. Perhaps Mom was right and James wanted to apologize, clear his conscience. Even though she had no intention of ever seeing him again, she could forgive him. It was the right thing to do.

"I can do that," she said. Tomorrow.

She started toward the door. "I'll see you at church in a couple of hours."

* * *

Caleb hummed as he dressed for church. What would it hurt to go? Church was just a bunch of people, most of whom he knew, singing songs and praying. He wouldn't die from it, and his attendance would make two people he cared about very happy. And that made him happy.

Pops had left earlier, having promised to help with preparations. Caleb worried that anything beyond the service was too much after today's treatment, but Pops had been so upbeat, his color better, that Caleb had kept his mouth shut.

He ran a comb through his hair, again, studying himself in the bathroom mirror. He was no catch, and he couldn't imagine what Kristen saw in him.

She sure had looked pretty today. She'd laughed when he'd said so, and twirled around, modeling a pair of black scrubs. He didn't care if she wore a tent. She'd still be beautiful. So he'd kissed her a couple of times while R2-D2 had cleaned Pops's blood.

Yeah, things were looking up.

He didn't own a tie, but the white shirt and black jeans with the black jacket he reserved for funerals and cattlemen's meetings looked okay. He slipped on the jacket, grabbed his wallet and keys, patted Rip on the head and headed out.

The snow had turned to slush and the country road was muddy with ruts. His truck wouldn't look too pretty, but it was dark. Maybe no one would notice.

In a few minutes, he'd be with Kristen. Anticipation flowed through his bloodstream, energizing him. He clicked on an all-Christmas radio station. Kristen played it every time she rode in his truck.

The church parking lot was already beginning to fill. He looked for Kristen's Honda and, not seeing it, decided to wait until she arrived. Walking into a strange place alone was awkward. Especially a church.

He watched the cars filing in from the street and making the circle around to the parking areas. Pickup trucks, SUVs, nice sedans and older cars, the norm in Refuge. A Maserati, however, was a rare sight. When the apple-red sports car made the circle and pulled into a parking spot, Caleb couldn't take his eyes off the sweet-looking ride. Any man would be mesmerized.

Refuge had its share of wealthy folks, but who owned a Maserati?

He must have been staring too hard at the unusual car to see Kristen arrive, because suddenly there she was, getting out of her Honda, her coat over one arm. Caleb exited his muddy truck and started in her direction just as the Maserati opened up. A fair-haired man stepped out, looking like a model for some fashion designer.

Caleb's heart gave a hard, painful thud. He recognized Maserati man from his photo on Kristen's phone. James Dudley III.

Kristen spotted the newcomer, too, and turned toward him.

Some primal beast roared inside Caleb. *No!*

He picked up his pace.

By now, Kristen had reached the doc's fancy car. She was talking, but he couldn't hear the words. The doc spoke, too, holding out a bouquet of flowers. Kristen accepted them, and suddenly, she was in his arms, kissing him.

Caleb stopped in midstride. Every inadequate thought he'd ever had surged in like a tsunami. This was the kind of man Kristen needed and deserved. And from the looks of things, Dr. Dudley was the man she wanted.

He spun on his boots and hurried to the truck. His chest hurt so bad he could barely breathe. He'd known this couldn't last. Hadn't his gut told him? Hadn't he tried to guard his feelings? But she'd been too wonderful, and he'd loved her for too long.

Mind swirling, he drove toward the ranch, seeing nothing except Kristen in another man's arms.

His cell phone pinged. Ever hopeful for a donor, he pulled off the road.

His belly dipped. The text was from Kristen. Where are you? Is everything all right?

Caleb stared at the text, aching, unsure, lost. Finally, he tapped in a few words, lies that shattered his last, best dream.

It was better this way. Better for her. Even if it broke him into little pieces.

The phone rang immediately after he hit Send. He let it go to voice mail, but, worried about missing a donor call, he typed in his password and listened.

It was Janey at the donor center, returning the call he'd made earlier in the day. His hopes soared. And then crashed like a hurricane against the rocks. The center had tested seven new prospects. No one matched.

He didn't listen to the rest. He tossed the phone on the seat and rested his head on the steering wheel.

This day couldn't get any worse.

Chapter Nine

"Missed you at church." Pops stood at the door of Caleb's bedroom in his Sunday best.

Caleb lay on top of the covers, staring at the walls, still dressed up as if he had somewhere to go. "Changed my mind."

"When I left here you were on top of the world, eager to see Kristen, halfway excited about church."

Caleb sat up on the side of the bed, knocked over one of his polished boots. Rip lifted his head, made sure no attack was underway and lay down again. "Was."

"Want to a talk about it?" Pops lowered himself to the only chair in the room. He looked drained.

"I changed my mind. That's all." No use crying over it. Pops had way more problems than a broken heart. "You should go to bed. You don't look so hot."

"And you don't get dressed up like that to feed calves. Kristen looked real pretty, too."

The vision of her had lingered in Caleb's head all the way home. She'd looked gorgeous, shiny auburn hair swept back on one side and flowing over the shoulders of a bright blue dress. Tiptoeing up on strappy high heels to kiss another man.

"Let it go, Pops. I'm not the right guy for her. She deserves better."

"Is that what this is all about?"

Caleb rubbed both hands over his face. They smelled of aftershave, the kind Kristen liked. "Why stick around when the writing is on the wall? She's in another class. Educated, socially inclined, from a great family."

"Don't let the best thing in your life get away because you're too prideful to take a risk. You and Kristen Andrews were made for each other."

Dialysis must be going to Pops's head.

"She wants someone else."

"You know this for a fact?"

"Why wouldn't she? He's everything I'm not—smart, rich, good-looking, drives a Maserati."

Pops made a huffing sound. "You saying Kristen's not worth fighting for?"

"Of course, she is, but—"

"No *buts* about it, son. Don't be a foolish, stubborn man like I was. A woman like Kristen isn't going to choose a man for his car. She'll choose him for his heart."

Caleb knew that was true. It was his heart he was having trouble with. "She wants a man whose beliefs match hers."

"You believe in God, don't you?"

"Any fool cowboy who makes his living outdoors knows there's a God. All he has to do is open his eyes. But I'm not sure God cares much about what happens down here."

"If He didn't care, He wouldn't have sent his only Son to die in our place."

Caleb couldn't argue that. "But if God cares so much, why doesn't He make you well? Or at least send you a donor?"

"Well, now, son, God never promised to do those things. He's not a vending machine God that you can punch in a prayer and take out the answers that suit you. Fact is, faith isn't even about getting what we want from God. It's about trusting Him no matter what."

Pops gripped the sides of the chair and rose. His arms trembled, a sight that tormented Caleb.

"I want you well, Pops."

"My trust is in the Lord. Whatever He decides is fine with me. I want His decision to be fine with you, too." The older cowboy patted him on the shoulder. "Don't let my situation keep you from God. Or from Kristen."

While Caleb absorbed the words, Pops walked slowly out of the room.

Caleb stuck his feet in his boots.

With Rip tagging merrily along, he made his way outside and across the mushy ground, ruining the polish on his dress boots. After a quick look at a slowpoke heifer, he checked on the orphaned calf. He could almost see Kristen sitting there, on that upturned bucket, feeding the growing animal. She'd thought it great fun and hugged the little calf, naming her Jasmine. Crazy, amazing woman. Beef ranchers didn't name their cattle.

On the way back to the house, he stopped on the porch to stare at the stars. God was up there somewhere.

Faith isn't even about getting what we want from God, he thought, mulling Pops's words. *It's about trusting Him no matter what.*

How could he do that? As a boy, he'd believed in Jesus, and look what that had gotten him.

A light went on in the house. Pops was in the kitchen.

"Pops," he said softly, and another light came on, this one inside Caleb.

He'd prayed for a family and ended up with Pops, the finest man he knew. Was that God's doing?

Suddenly, a dozen important moments in his life sprang to memory. The woman at the truck stop restaurant who'd fed him ice cream and sat with him when it was clear his mother would not return. The social worker who'd enrolled him in Pops's mentoring program. The math teacher who'd tutored him after school. The teenage girl who'd plunked her lunch tray down beside his that first awful day at Refuge High. He'd been the only kid at the table, a stringy-haired trouble-maker dying inside. Then suddenly there was the cutest cheerleader in school, befriending him, chattering away as if they were friends. And once Kristen accepted him, others followed.

Why hadn't he seen that before?

His parents may have abandoned him, but God hadn't. He'd put people in his path and brought him to this Christmas Eve.

"I'm a mess, Jesus," he told the twinkling stars and the ink-black sky, "and I'm sorry about that. Sorry for being a jerk. Sorry for doubting you, for saying stupid things. I can't promise I won't stumble, but if you'll help me, I'll try to do better."

He focused on one star, imagining God there with His only Son. Imagining all those years ago on Christmas Eve when Jesus came as a help-less baby to a world that would someday mock and kill him.

Caleb didn't need a preacher to tell him what

a marvelous gift that was. He'd only needed to open his heart.

Grateful and touched, Caleb remained beneath the heavens until his body shook with cold and Rip nudged at his hand to go inside.

Circumstances hadn't changed. Pops was still dying. Kristen still belonged to another man. His heart still ached so badly he knew he would never heal. But deep down in his soul, Caleb finally felt at peace.

Kristen drove from the church to her apartment, but couldn't bring herself to go inside. The service had been beautiful as always and she'd basked in the quiet reverence of the worship and remembrance of a holy night that had changed the world. But she'd been troubled, too, praying to understand what could have happened with Caleb.

His text had been terse, almost cruel. I'm not the marrying kind. It's better to end this now. Be happy.

Was he crazy? How could she be happy after reading that? Had she so completely misunderstood him, the way she had James?

She rubbed the sharp pain beneath her breastbone. Part of her wanted to cry. Another part was concerned and still another was just plain mad. Wasn't it bad enough that James had shown up at the church with the worst idea ever?

Something was wrong. She just knew it. Things had been wonderful between her and Caleb earlier today. What had happened in the time between?

"I'm never going to get to sleep anyway." She grabbed her phone, shot him a text. I'm on my way over. Deal with it.

Then she put the car in Reverse and drove down some of the muddiest roads in the county to the Girard ranch. A light was on inside the house, the Christmas tree they'd decorated together visible in the window. It wasn't that late. He was still up.

She marched to the door and lifted her hand to knock. The door opened and there stood the cowboy of her dreams, scowling.

She pushed her way right past him and went into the living room. "If you have something to say to me, say it to my face. Texting is the coward's way."

He stacked both hands on his hips, his expression dangerous. "You might be the only person who could get away with calling me a coward."

She marched up to him, close enough that his eyes widened. "Why is that?"

He opened his mouth, closed it again.

"Because you love me?" There. She'd tossed

down the gauntlet. If he threw it back in her face, she'd be devastated, but at least she'd know what was going on.

She yanked her coat off and tossed it on the couch. Rip nudged at her hand. She ignored him. "Talk, Caleb. I'm not leaving here until you tell me what is going on in that head of yours."

"I don't know what you mean."

Greg stuck his head around the end of the hallway. "Yes, you do, boy. She's worth it. So are you. Now, get on with it. I'm going to bed."

In seconds a door slammed, but Kristen's focus was on Caleb.

Finally, he said, "I saw you with Maserati man."

Oh, so that was it.

"You were there? At the church?"

"Parking lot."

"You should have stayed."

"I'm not that into self-punishment."

"James was a surprise. Not a pleasant one. And I told him so."

He shoved his hands in his pockets, unyielding. "Didn't look that way to me."

"You saw him kiss me. Is that it?"

"I'm not a complete fool, Kristen. He's everything you want in a man. Brilliant, successful, charming. All the nurses were after him but you won. Those are your own words. Now the good doctor has driven all the way from Colorado to see you. It's pretty obvious you belong together. You don't have to play nice to save my feelings. I wish you the best."

"Get this straight, cowboy." She poked him in the chest. "James kissed me. I did not kiss him. His was a totally unexpected move that caught me off balance. What you saw was me holding on to keep from falling and ruining my new dress in the nasty slush."

"He's perfect for you, Kristen." His voice was soft now, almost tender. "Whatever you think we have is nothing compared to what he can give you. I won't stand in your way. You deserve him."

She gave him a long look, her world spinning out from under her. Caleb wasn't falling in love with her after all. But he was too kind to say so. Was that it? Was he bearing the load, letting her down easy, giving her an out through James, letting her save face by taking the blame?

She felt like a complete fool.

"I know what you're trying to do," she said. "But nothing you say can change the way I feel about you, the way I've probably always felt about you. I wish it could."

She grabbed her coat and went to the door, defeated. Now she knew. Now she would have to forget the teenage boy who'd grown to be the man she loved.

They'd barely begun. And now it was over.

* * *

Caleb stood like a statue, his whole world crumbling around him. She'd left him. He'd known she would eventually. That was why he'd tried not to love her.

He followed her to the door, saying nothing, letting her walk out of his life, the way she should. "You were made for better things."

She glared at him and started down the steps.

He wanted to beg her to stay. Nothing made sense without her. Not anymore.

Pops's advice floated through him. *Don't let the best thing in your life get away because you're too prideful to take a risk.*

Blood began to pound in Caleb's ears. He knew what risk Pops meant. The risk of rejection. It was a cancer in Caleb's life. Always had been. The fear that he was never enough, certainly not for Kristen.

The bitter root pushed up, telling him he'd been right. She hadn't stayed.

He pushed back. Her leaving was his fault, not hers.

"Kristen!" The word shot out, unbidden. She whirled, a shadow beyond his porch light. "Don't go."

Her shoulders sagged. "Give me one good reason."

He stepped off the porch. She took a step away, eyeing him with a wounded expression.

He'd hurt her, fool that he was. Was he too late? "I messed up. I'm sorry. Forgive me."

"For what?" Her shoulders were stiff, but her voice quavered. "Being honest enough to tell me you don't want me?"

"Not want you? Are you crazy? I want you so much, I can't think straight." He clenched his fist over his heart and blurted out the words he'd longed to say for years. "I love you, Kristen. I can't breathe without you." His voice fell to a whisper. He reached out a hand. "Don't leave me. Please don't leave."

Her face crumpled. Was she crying? In the next second, she was in his arms. He didn't know how it happened, but he was holding her, kissing her, and she was kissing him, tears running down her cheeks. The fear inside him melted. Kristen melted him.

When they finally came up for air, he whispered, "Beautiful face. Don't cry."

She caught his hands with hers and asked, hurt in her tone, "Why did you send me away?"

"I shouldn't have. It was stupid. I was afraid."

"Of me?"

"Afraid you couldn't really love me. Afraid that you'd come to your senses if the doc came back around. I'm not good enough for you. I know that."

"Oh, Caleb." She touched his cheek. "Sweet Caleb. I love you so much."

"You deserve a guy who can buy you flowers and fancy cars and ski trips, not an uneducated cowpuncher like me."

She gripped his chin between her fingers. "Stop it. I don't need trips or cars or flowers. I need you." She gave his chin a shake. "*You.* Caleb Girard. I. Love. You. Get used to it."

The wonder of it overwhelmed him. "You'd choose me over him?"

"You're twice the man he is," she said with an indignant little huff.

He found that hard to believe.

"You know why he came here?"

"Why?"

"To tell me he had forgiven me for my behavior at the ski lodge and to ask me to move in with him. As long as I didn't interfere with his social life. No wedding. No declarations of love. Just pack up and go to his condo and make up for lost time."

Caleb growled low in his throat, feeling as feral as a wolf. "He said that?"

"He thought I'd be over myself by now and excited to have him back. After all, he's a great catch, and why would I want to be stuck in this provincial little town when I could be with him?"

"He has a point."

"He does not! And I told him so. I also told him to go home and never contact me again. I don't love him. Never did. I just wanted to. It took coming home to you to realize what love really means."

Something settled inside Caleb, as if his world at last was centered and right. He'd waited a lifetime for Kristen. And she was finally home, finally in his arms with love in her words and in her eyes.

Pulling her close against the cold, he gazed up at the Milky Way and whispered, "Thank you."

"You're welcome," she whispered back.

His heart was so full, his joy so complete, he laughed, lifted her off the ground and swung her in a circle. The cold air stirred around them, but Caleb was too warm inside to notice.

Kristen was laughing, her head tilted back, so that they almost missed the sound of their cell phones. Both of them. Ringing at the same time.

He grappled for his phone just as it stopped ringing. Before he could hit redial, Kristen's eyes flashed to his, widening as she held the phone to her ear. Caleb's pulse picked up.

When the call ended, she broke into a smile,

threw her arms out wide and cried, "We've got a match!"

Caleb held her close, rejoicing, thanking God with such passion he thought his heart would explode.

"A miracle," he murmured against Kristen's coconut-scented hair.

He hadn't believed before, but now he knew, God not only answered prayers, He sometimes answered them exactly as hoped.

Epilogue

Seven weeks later, after the most wonderful Christmas of her life, Kristen stood beside Greg's hospital bed with her favorite cowboy.

"You look great," she told the patient.

"Doc says the transplant went better than expected, no signs of rejection." He winked at Caleb. "Funny how God worked everything out. Pretty nice Christmas gift."

"Can't argue that." Caleb's voice was soft but firm.

"God is good." Then he added, "No matter what."

Kristen had been ecstatic to learn of Caleb's renewed faith. She'd known all along he believed. He just had to realize it.

He was such a fine man. She saw it in the work he did, the way he faithfully mentored five troubled boys, the way he looked after her as if she was his most precious treasure. He said she was, and she believed him.

God had answered her prayers, too.

"You two need to go home and get some rest," Pops said. "Son, you look like the end of a bad road."

"I'm fine, Pops," Caleb said, though he had to be exhausted.

Other than quick trips home to feed animals, her cowboy had spent every day and night at the hospital with his dad. His love and respect for Greg was only one of the many reasons she loved him so much.

"Set the date yet?"

"Pops!" Caleb grinned at her and shook his head. "Must be the anesthesia."

She circled her cowboy's waist with both arms, leaning close, smiling.

They'd talked about the future, but since Christmas, they'd been so busy and so happy basking in their newfound love, they'd made no plans. Soon, though. Soon.

"Your transplant had to come first, Greg."

"Now it's done. So get the show on the road. I want to teach my grandkids how to ride and rope."

She laughed. "You've got my parents wishing for grandchildren, too. But not yet, please. I want your son all to myself for a while."

To Kristen's relief, her parents weren't upset that she'd chosen a hometown cowboy. Mom had only wanted to be sure she wouldn't regret her decision about James. Once she'd witnessed Caleb's devotion and her daughter's joy, she'd embraced the cowboy and his dad like family.

She squeezed Caleb's arm and gazed up into his beloved face with all the love she had inside. A mountain of love.

Life hadn't turned out the way she'd planned. It had turned out better.

Caleb built a fire in the fireplace, grateful to be home. Tonight he could rest. Pops was doing great. He could stop worrying.

"Thanks for making me come home."

Kristen stood at his side, handing him logs. "You're exhausted. I can't have you getting sick on me. I love you."

Best words ever. She couldn't say them often enough. Some days, he pinched himself, amazed that Kristen could love him. But she did.

"Plus," she said, trailing a hand over his shoulder, "we needed some alone time."

"I like the sound of that." He lit the fire and rose, taking her in his arms. He rocked her back and forth, heart full of gratitude. For Pops's transplant. For God's transforming power. For her.

He could hardly wrap his head around the changes his Christmas miracle had brought.

"A month ago, I was lost and broken," he murmured, leaning back to look into the face of the woman who loved him, "certain I'd never find peace and just as certain I'd never find love. It feels so good to be wrong."

"I was broken, too." She caressed his face, her hands tender. "But I didn't know it until you came back into my life, the man I've always loved, the man who completes me."

The flames rose, warming them, but no fire could burn as brightly as the love he'd found in her.

Together, Kristen and God had done the impossible. They'd healed him. And he'd never again doubt that miracles happened. He knew they did, because they'd happened to him.

* * * * *

FALLING FOR THE CHRISTMAS COWBOY

Ruth Logan Herne

To my beautiful friend Catherine Hoffman, a woman I admire and respect and love to call my friend…may your days be rich and full and may every Christmas with those beautiful children bring you faith, hope and love.

But after that the kindness and love of God our Savior toward man appeared, Not by works of righteousness which we have done, but according to his mercy he saved us, by the washing of regeneration, and renewing of the Holy Ghost; Which he shed on us abundantly through Jesus Christ our Savior; That being justified by his grace, we should be made heirs according to the hope of eternal life.

—*Titus* 3:4–7

Chapter One

❧

Twelve insensible heifers were all that stood between Ty Carrington and a delicious roasted turkey. He pulled his scarf tight against the western Idaho winds and faced the other two ranch hands. "Let's get this done."

"I'll go right," offered George, one of their original cowboys on the ranch.

"I've got left." Billy was already backing his horse up to take the far curve.

"And I'll circle from above," Ty told them. The bite of the northwest wind should be enough inducement to get the first years down to the lower pasture quickly, but the thought of that dinner…

Roasted free-range turkey. Two kinds of stuffing. Mashed potatoes. Sweet potatoes. Cranberry-orange relish. Homemade rolls. Corn casserole. Platters of meat and deep bowls of gravy, with more desserts than any spread should allow. Carrington Acres looked out for their people. His family expected an honest day's work but took care of folks in return.

Holidays made him think.

Ty didn't want to think. Didn't want to remember. Didn't want to ponder life's realities unless it had to do with cows or horses.

They triple-teamed the remaining stragglers, and when the last young cow was safely tucked in on the near side of the lower field, Ty latched the first gate.

Done.

The sharp wind froze his cheeks beneath a five-day beard. Over 250 heifers that were scheduled for winter deliveries were now closer to the barns. He'd just latched the last gate when his cell phone rang. Effie Broderick's name showed up on the screen. Effie was an old gal who lived in the tiny village of Shepherd's Crossing. "Miss Effie." He climbed down from his horse and began to walk her toward the front barn. "Happy Thanksgiving to you." He didn't say it because he cared about the holiday—he didn't—but it was the polite thing to do. "This is a surprise."

"I know the truth in that, Ty, because I don't think I've ever placed a call to Carrington Acres before, but there's something going on here in town, and, with Eric away, I figured you'd be the best one to handle it."

What could possibly be going wrong in Shepherd's Crossing? The sorry little town had sat half-empty since he'd arrived five years ago. He walked at a steady pace, letting the dun mare cool down. "What's up?"

"Someone's in one of the houses."

"The houses?" He played dumb to gather his bearings because he knew exactly what she meant. When the neighboring ranch owners had recently pushed to put the town back together again, he and his brother Eric had made the decision to purchase several of the empty buildings in town. Every one of the buildings was vacant, so there shouldn't be people in them. "Which one, Effie? And are you sure?" If someone had taken up residence in one of the foreclosed places, they'd need to move. Those houses had been bought and paid for. The thought of squatters didn't sit well.

"Sure as shootin'," she replied. "They're staying in the faded green one on Harrison."

Ty knew the house. The county had taken it due to lack of tax payment. The Carringtons had purchased it fair and square. "I'll come straight in and check it out."

He remounted the horse. Hadn't he been lamenting that the mare hadn't been exercised enough the last few weeks? A ride into town would fix that.

He told the other men where he was going and headed north. They'd have put Lady up for him and he could have grabbed the Jeep, but there was something solid about a Thanksgiving ride. He drew her to a halt near one of the old hitching posts in town, tied her off and cut across the narrow street.

Effie was right. There were lights on in the green house. He climbed the two worn steps and rapped sharply on the door. He half expected whoever it was to hide themselves because they weren't supposed to be there, so when an absolutely beautiful young woman opened the door, Ty wasn't sure what to trip over first—his surprise or his words. Dark hair, long and wavy, framed a classic face with high cheekbones and a perfect smile. He wasn't sure of her heritage, but in the world of genetics, she'd got the cream of the crop. Bright brown eyes sparkled as she leaned the storm door open.

"Hello." She aimed a soft smile at him. "Can I help you?"

"I hope so, ma'am." He removed his tan cowboy hat and put it over his chest the way a gentleman would, except most gentlemen didn't throw people to the curb on Thanksgiving. "I'm Ty Carrington. I've got a ranch outside of town."

She nodded as he spoke.

"This house here? The one you're in?"

"I know it's a little rough around the edges, but we'll make do," she assured him. "When spring comes, Dovie and I will have so much fun making a garden. Maybe trimming the lawn, but maybe not. We'll see." She pulled her hoodie closer. "Would you like to come in? That wind is sharp."

He felt funny going inside, but she wasn't dressed for the outdoors. He stepped across the threshold. "I'm afraid there's been a misunderstanding."

"Oh?" She shut the door and faced him. "How so?"

"This house."

She nodded. "My aunt Celia's place. She left it to me nearly two years ago." Her gaze clouded slightly. "Circumstances didn't allow me to get up here and see it until just now. But we rolled in last night with plenty of time to get settled over the winter. I was surprised that the utilities were still turned on, but grateful. I didn't have to do a single thing except turn the key and hit a light switch. And we'll have to clean, of course. But that's to be expected."

"Of course. Ma'am, it's just that—"

"Mommy! Do we have company? Isn't this the most special day ever?" A tiny version of the woman skipped out from the back of the house. She sported even darker hair, only hers was in twin ponytails that bounced with every movement. Dark eyes, crinkled in laughter, sparkled up at him.

"Come here, Dovie." She picked up the little girl and faced him. "My daughter, Mary White Dove Lambert. I'm Jessica Lambert. Welcome to our home."

"See, that's just it." Ty raked his hand across the nape of his neck. "I don't think this is your home."

She frowned. "Of course it is. My aunt's attorney sent me all the paperwork to transfer ownership when she passed away."

"And what did you do with the paperwork?" he asked.

She frowned. "What do you mean?"

"The transfer of ownership. Did you sign the papers? Send them back? Pay the taxes?"

She held the little girl closer. Tighter. "Of course I did. Well, the paperwork, anyway. To the county, actually, not a place here in town. I kept copies for myself. I don't understand what you're saying."

"No one paid the taxes on this property for over two years. The county let it go for lack of tax payment a few weeks ago. Our ranch purchased this property and several others here in town."

"That's impossible."

Right now he wished it were. "Are you sure you're in the right house?"

She nailed him with a straight-on look. "Do you think my aunt's key would work in other doors? Or are you suggesting we broke in?"

"No, ma'am. And it's Thanksgiving. I didn't come by to cause any problems. But this is Carrington property, so I'm going to have to ask you to move by Monday."

"You don't really think that I'm going to let you turn myself and my four-year-old daughter out into the cold because of some weird county mix-up, do you?" The little girl had looked so happy to have company. Now she looked suspicious. And worried.

Great, he'd managed to distress a little kid on Thanksgiving. Had five years of running herd and avoiding people robbed him of even the slightest bit of common sense? Jessica pulled open the door. "You need to leave."

"I will." The last thing he wanted to do was cause a problem for her, but he understood the law. This house—no matter who she thought she got it from—was a Carrington house now. As he turned toward the door, he spotted a square wooden table beyond the living room. A tiny roasted bird the size of a game hen stood, ready to carve. An equally small bowl of potatoes sat off to the side. And peas.

That was it.

That was the sum of their Thanksgiving dinner.

Not your fault. Everything bad that happens in the world is not your fault.

He stepped outside. She shut the door firmly behind him and clicked the lock.

Lady stamped her foot, an equine message that she'd been waiting long enough for him.

He rode her back to the ranch nice and easy. If he was late for dinner, that was all right. He'd miss the praying and the thanking part of it, and they were probably all better off for that. His current brand of cynicism wasn't meant for Thanksgiving tables. Or altars. Or pulpits. Yeah, he'd be fine to miss the thanking part.

As long as there was hot turkey and a few slices of bread, he'd make do, but when he got the mare put up and entered the kitchen, amazing scents accosted him. Sally Ann had gone the distance to make the crew a beautiful meal, but all he could think about was that Cornish game hen sitting on a worn table next to a bowl of round green peas.

And he'd just kicked her out of the house.

A good share of Jessica Lambert's ancestors may have been relegated to a reservation, but that was in the distant past. She was a modern

Native American mix and this was her house. Her place. And she was willing to take on anyone who tried to say otherwise, even unshaven cowboys sporting short, curly blond hair and big blue eyes. Clearly there was a mistake, one that she'd clear up on Monday. End of story.

"Who was that man, Mommy?" Dovie framed Jessica's cheeks with her two small hands. "And why did he make you sad?"

"Not sad, Dovie. What rhymes with *sad*?" Jessica asked. She set the girl down and moved toward the table.

"Bad! Glad! Mad!" she recited, ticking off her fingers. "That's such an easy one, Mommy."

"Because you're such a smart girl," Jessica told her. "And our dinner is ready, although I need to warm up the potatoes and peas in the microwave. Let me get that done and we can pray together."

"And then we have a Thanksgiving feast!" Dovie scrambled into one of the three chairs and waited while Jessica warmed the vegetables.

A four-year-old's palate was easily satisfied. Anything could be a feast. As long as Jessica pushed herself to view things through Dovie's eyes and not society's perceptions, they'd do all right.

But what about that man? Ty Carrington? Could his ranch truly have a claim on this house?

No.

She'd done everything she was supposed to do. The fact that the county had never sent her a tax bill couldn't be considered her fault. Yet, maybe she should have looked into it further...

Be kind to yourself. You've had a lot on your plate. Have dinner. Watch a movie. Talk about faith, hope and love.

She brought the potatoes and peas back to the table.

Dovie sat up straighter. She leaned over and drew a deep breath. "Doesn't this smell so very good, Mommy?"

"Wonderfully good," said Jessica. She sat down and took her daughter's hand. "Let's each tell God something we're thankful for this year. Okay?"

Dovie, never one to shirk the limelight, nodded quickly. "God, I'm so happy with our new house! Thank You so much for it, and thank You for this good food." She looked at Jessica, expectant. "Your turn, Mommy!"

"Dear Lord, I, too, am thankful for this sweet home. A warm fire. And, most of all, my Lovie-Dovie."

"Oh, Mom!" Dovie giggled like she did every time Jessica called her Lovie-Dovie. So sweet. So trusting.

Jessica understood that the world was not always to be trusted. She'd learned some hard lessons, but she'd also learned when to back down and when to hold her ground.

She'd come north from the Nebraska–South Dakota border to claim this inheritance. Away from her late husband's home and family. Away from the troubles of the reservation he so badly wanted to help. That goal had been cut short by his death over a year before.

She was a homeowner now.

And no one—no matter what they said or did—was going to take that from her.

were to be erased. She turned away hard too
once, but she'd also vowed never to break ties
and then at word of promise...

Chapter Two

"I don't see any stores here," Dovie said as she swung Jessica's arm when they walked through town midday Friday.

"Me, neither." Jessica pondered that as they completed their loop. "Most little towns have at least a couple of businesses."

"Where can we shop?"

She'd promised Dovie they'd go grocery shopping together, always a treat for the four-year-old. "Let's grab the car and we'll find food."

"And now we've got nice clean cupboards to put it in."

"We do." They'd scrubbed out the cupboards and the fridge with cleaning supplies she'd brought with them. She hadn't left Ben's family a forwarding address. They saw her as a turncoat.

She was nothing of the kind, but Dovie was her priority now. She could raise her to respect the dignity of her Native American heritage, but she wanted her to respect her European ancestry, too. That was no longer possible around Ben's family. Dark, simmering anger had overtaken them once Ben was gone. And greed.

She grabbed the car keys while Dovie fastened her seat belt around the booster seat. Then she climbed in and turned the key.

Nothing happened.

She frowned, gazing at the dashboard signals. She wasn't good with cars. She was good with computers. Graphics.

Car engines? Not so much.

She pulled out her cell phone to find a nearby repair shop.

There were no nearby repair shops. The closest ones were a half hour away, and they were both marked "Closed for Holiday Weekend."

This couldn't be happening. Nobody closed for the full weekend, did they?

She bit back panic and considered what they had on hand. A tiny portion of hen breast and half a stick of butter. They'd eaten the last of the bread for breakfast. She'd planned on shopping once they'd got to Idaho, but there had been long lines on the day before Thanksgiving, so she'd waited. Big mistake…

No people. No stores. No food. No car.

Now it was okay to panic.

A dusty green sedan rolled up and parked along the curb. A woman climbed out. She spotted Jessica in the car and waved to get her attention. Jess climbed out.

"Ty sent me over." The middle-aged Latina woman flashed Jess a broad smile as she came up the walk, carrying a large box. "Normally we have so many people on the ranch that we go through these leftovers fast."

"Leftovers?"

"From dinner yesterday. A fine feast, a blessed day. I'm Sally Ann Montroya. Or just Sally, either way. I'm from Carrington Acres. It's a ranch south of town. So nice to meet you!"

Food from the ranch that had purchased the empty houses in town. It was a kind gesture, but she wasn't poverty-stricken, just a little light in the wallet. No one had ever brought around charity baskets before, and embarrassment gripped her throat.

She led Sally Ann into the house and called for Dovie. When Dovie skipped up the steps after them, Jessica faced Sally Ann. "You said Ty sent you? The cowboy that wants me to give up my house?"

"What a mix-up!" Sally Ann didn't seem all that bothered, but, then, it wasn't her house on the line. "All will be straightened out, I'm sure, but for today so many good things right here. Were you going out?"

"We were going grocery shopping, but the car won't start and there's nowhere in town to even buy a quart of milk."

"So sad." Sally Ann widened her big brown eyes. "Not the milk—that we can fix—but the town, so empty, so forlorn, as if waiting for something, you know?"

No. Jessica did not know, but Sally's kindly nature made her almost want to know. "I cannot fix cars," said Sally, "and I'm heading to an appointment for my father. His chemotherapy is today and I sit with him. But I will drop off milk on my way back from McCall. It's the next town north of us, and it's bigger. What else do you need? I'll stop by the market and get it. It's right on my way."

"Really? Even after all this?" Jessica couldn't believe what was in the box: plastic containers of turkey and gravy, potatoes, beans, squash, a full apple pie and half a pumpkin pie. "This is amazing."

"We'll figure out your car and the house and everything," Sally Ann promised. "I'll let Ty know. He and the other men are up in the hills today, but he'll be back down by morning. He'll fix it." She indicated the car with a thrust of her chin. "But, of course, I need your phone number." She entered Jessica's number into her phone, then bustled toward the door. She paused long enough to touch Dovie's head and give her a blessing, then hurried to the green car. She made a U-turn, honked the horn, then headed back toward old 95.

In the space of five minutes, conditions had changed from needy to blessed, and not by her hands.

God's hands. And the kindness of strangers.

So this cowboy had done a nice thing. A really nice thing. But that didn't mean she was giving up her house. Not without a fight. A fight she *had* to win.

Sally Ann's text came through on Saturday, one of the trials of being in the high country. Cell coverage was solid in the valley, but once you went into the hills, nada. When Ty heard the pinging of missed texts, a part of him longed to turn right around and go back uphill.

He didn't. He'd moved somewhat beyond the anger that used to grip him daily.

Now, as long as he kept God out of the equation, he didn't feel like such a failure.

He put the phone away. He'd answer the texts from Eric and Sally Ann later. Few others texted him. Few knew where he was or what he was doing. And every year, around this time, when folks began singing about decking halls and being jolly, all he could think of were empty seats at family tables. Including his. And his heart wanted to break all over again.

By the time he scrolled through the texts early that evening, one stood out: Jessica in green house. Her car is not working. Needs food. Needs help.

Typical Sally Ann, looking out for others, but she had a lot to handle with her father's illness. She'd added Jessica's number. He texted the number. Car repair shops are all closed until Monday. I'll come take a look tomorrow.

He wasn't sure she'd answer. When she did, he could almost feel the reluctance in her words. I'd appreciate it.

Nine o'clock okay?

Church service is at nine, she texted back. After that.

There was no church service in Shepherd's Crossing anymore. Declining health had forced the aged pastor to retire back in June. Folks had put together weekly services since then because there was no replacement pastor. And until they had money to pay a salary, there wouldn't be one. But he didn't mention that. She'd find out soon enough. Around ten, then.

He'd drive in, figure out what was going on with the car and get things moving for her. Bad enough she was going to have to leave the house she thought she owned…but to do so without a car?

That went beyond unfair.

A text came in from her. With a picture attached, of her and the little girl feasting on apple pie. Pie: it's what's for breakfast.

He smiled. He couldn't help it. He loved pie for breakfast. He'd loved all kinds of normal, everyday things. Until…

He texted back, Perfect way to start the day.

Whatever the new week brought, he'd be on hand to help figure things out. She'd need a car to check with the county about the house. And to shop for groceries. He couldn't exactly lend her Eric's jazzed-up sports car, and Eric had taken his SUV to the Colorado pharmaceutical plant. The cows had all been taken to freshened pastures. Until calves started dropping in early February, they were in the slower months of the year, which meant he had time to add chauffeur to his job list for the next couple of days.

A final text came through, another selfie, this time just of her and a forkful of delicious apple pie. Or the perfect bedtime snack… Thank you!

He'd felt guilt ridden all day Thursday, and if he'd had time to help her himself, he'd have done it. Seeing a single mother in trouble hit him wrong.

He smiled at the text and the picture.

She had to be worried about the future, and yet her smile was nonchalant.

He drew off his gear and put it in the mudroom, readily available, an old habit from being called out at night on a regular basis. For human crises. Crises of the heart. Crises of the soul. Beginnings and endings. He'd sat and prayed over both and everything in between.

Now his callouts were bovine related, and not so often, and frankly he found the occasional cow crisis far easier to deal with than anything human related back east.

Chapter Three

"I love living in a place where we can walk to church, Mommy!" Dovie swung Jessica's hand as they strolled up Harrison Street toward the old clapboard-and-stone church.

"Very nice," she agreed, but something was wrong. There were no cars filtering into the village and parking near the church. There were no other people walking down the street for the nine o'clock service, and yet she was sure that was what the sign had indicated. As they drew close, a burst of wind sent Dovie's hat flying.

"Eek!" She laughed and clapped her hands over her head while Jessica chased down the errant hat. "That wind is just like Nebraska wind!"

"It sure is, which leaves me to wonder why Aunt Celia couldn't have fallen in love with a man from, say, Texas? New Mexico? Or a crooner from Tennessee?"

"What's a crooner?" Dovie wondered, as they climbed the stairs. When Jessica tried the church door and found it locked, Dovie frowned. "Doesn't anybody else want to go to church, Mommy?" She glanced back and forth, as if hoping someone would show up. "Are we all alone?"

"Of course not, honey, I'm sure there are other people living nearby," she told her, but now that they'd been here a couple of days, she wasn't nearly as certain.

The town wasn't exactly desolate. A few cars had made their way in and out the past couple of days. But just a few.

She was about to start back home when a car pulled up. Then another. And another.

Half a dozen cars rolled in, all coming from the same direction, and when one of the gentlemen proffered a key, Dovie clapped her hands in glee. "We do have a church in this town, Mommy! We do!"

"Running late as usual, but we haven't had anyone waiting for us before now, so that will push us to be on time." A dark-skinned older woman came up the stairs and extended her hand. "I am Cora Lee Satterly from Pine Ridge Ranch. It is a most certainly a pleasure to make your acquaintance."

"Jessica Lambert." Jessica took her hand and

smiled. "That sweet drawl wasn't at all what I expected," she added. "You're Southern."

"Guilty as charged. But living up north now. And happy to be here," she finished as several other people came up the steps. The first man—tall, square shouldered and good-looking—put the key in the lock, and when the door swung open, he grinned. "Every week I'm pretty sure that old lock's going to fail us. And every week we make it in."

"I'm putting this sweet church on my rehab list," said a dark-haired young woman holding a blonde baby girl. "Maybe we can find ourselves a pastor that way."

"There's no pastor?" Jessica asked, looking around as other folks arrived.

"When ours retired, there was no one to take his place," said the man with the key. "Heath Caufield," he continued, introducing himself, then slipped an arm around the woman at his side. "My wife, Lizzie. And our son, Zeke."

"And a host of other local folks," said an older gentleman. "We do our own prayer service in the meantime. Kind of nice, actually. It takes us back to when folks first settled these parts, before a town was a town. With God's blessing and a little time, we'll make it a town once again." He patted Dovie on the head and she preened. "Welcome to Shepherd's Crossing, little lady."

"Thank you!" She smiled up at him, delighted that more people had come. So was Jessica. But a town with so few people? A town with one untended church?

Before she sank deep roots into this rich Idaho soil, she was going to make sure this was the kind of place to raise a child. A child should have friends to play with. A school to attend. And churches with pealing bells on Sunday morning.

As if on cue, the bell tower began chiming above her. The rich metallic tones called out loud and clear, and the little boy—Zeke, they'd called him—fist punched the air.

"My favorite thing," he exclaimed, then clamped his hands over his mouth. "Sorry, Dad." He sent an *oops!* look to his father. "I forgot to be quiet."

The bells calmed.

A prayerful silence ensued, and then the older gentleman went forward and read Bible passages. No music. No organ.

You play piano. You could volunteer. There's an old keyboard right over there.

She didn't offer. If it was just her, then sure. She could make do.

But this wasn't just her. It was Dovie's childhood, Dovie's memories they were talking about. All she'd ever wanted was for her children to live in a place unclouded by addiction and greed. A place filled with goodness and love. To do for her daughter what her mother had done for her so long ago, before an unexpected heart attack had tugged Mary Lambert from this earth.

She didn't linger when the service came to a close. She took Dovie's hand and started down the steps. Maybe she shouldn't fight losing the house. She was a talented graphic designer. She could work from home anywhere and make enough to get by.

"Jessica?"

She turned. Lizzie Caufield was coming down the steps toward her. "Yes?"

"Where are you living? Are you close by?"

Jessica nodded toward Harrison Street. "The third house in. I inherited it from my late aunt."

Lizzie's brow wrinkled slightly, but she didn't ask questions. "Welcome." Lizzie offered her a warm smile. "We were rushing earlier, but we'd love to have you come out to Pine Ridge Ranch. Zeke would be over the moon to have a playmate visit and we can show you some old-fashioned Southern hospitality."

"While we try to find out as much about you as we can," added another woman. Her honesty made Jessica smile.

"I like women who know how to keep their priorities straight," she replied.

"We're all there today if you're available," Lizzie said.

Jessica felt funny admitting her car wasn't running. She shook her head. "I've got a freelance book-cover project due tomorrow, so I've got to finesse things before it goes out to a client."

Lizzie's eyes went wide. "You do graphic design?"

"I love graphics," she admitted. "I've always loved creating things, and computer design has opened up so many doors for me."

"And you're living here? You're not just visiting?" Lizzie Caufield didn't look simply happy. She looked excited.

The other woman leaned in slightly. "You're scaring her, Lizzie. Might want to tone it down. I'm Melonie, by the way. Her sister. The sane one."

Jessica laughed as others came out of the church and gathered around them. "Yes and yes. Are you in need of graphics?"

"If we start a small-town newspaper, I am," declared Lizzie. "Now you've got to come by. I'm all thumbs with layered effects and fonts, but I've got a great hand with writing. We'll talk, all right?"

Jessica nodded. "I'll look forward to it." She gave Lizzie her business card, and as quickly as the little town had filled with a few dozen people, it emptied.

She and Dovie walked back to the house down lonely, quiet streets. Too quiet.

They'd just started up the walk when a white Jeep rolled to the curb. Ty Carrington climbed out and came her way. "If you toss me your keys, I'll see if I can get this car running. It's a tough place to be caught without transportation, especially with no grocery store on hand."

"And no church, school, library…"

"Folks have left. But there are new folks in town, and they've got hopes to make things better." He shrugged lightly. "It might be too little, too late. But then again, maybe not."

Jessica hadn't bargained on the lack of townspeople. The lack of simple business support. The thought of an emergency with Dovie, and so little around…

She indicated the broken car. "This is kind of you, but it's not really your worry."

"Well, ma'am, see, that's just it." He sent her a gaze of such sweet sincerity that it was like a welcome home. "If nothing else, we should all be kind. Right?"

"I'm cold, Mommy."

He moved toward her car. "Toss me those keys and I'll give this a once-over."

She didn't want to take help from him. From anyone, really. But maybe especially from the guy trying to throw her out of her house.

Having said that, she had a child to feed and no way to get food, which meant she needed his help even if she didn't want to take it. She tossed him the keys and took Dovie inside.

He came to the door about ten minutes later and shook his head. "Nothing I can fix, I'm afraid. It looks like it needs a trip to a well-equipped repair shop, and the closest one is down in Council. We've got a tow truck at the ranch. I can come by tomorrow, hook this up and get it down there for you. Save you the cost of a tow."

"You can't be expected to do that for free," she argued, but he shrugged that off.

"It's our quiet season, there's help on hand and I've got the equipment. Happy to help, ma'am."

"Jessica."

He waited.

"Don't call me ma'am and go all cute cowboy on me. My name is Jessica."

"A pleasure to meet you again, Jessica." His quick grin tried to melt her heart. She resisted, but just barely. Someone had once said keep your friends close and your enemies closer.

Anyone trying to take her house out from under her fitted the latter, even though he had the sweetest blue eyes she'd ever seen.

"I've got a few hours. Plenty of time to make a grocery run. If you need a loan…"

"Money's not a problem." She pulled the door open to let him in. "I just didn't realize that nothing would be available locally and should have stopped along the way. Now I know better."

"I've been *dying* to go shopping," Dovie said dramatically to Ty. "I have, like, a *whole list* of things we need to put in our nice, clean cupboards, so that would be fun, right? If we all go together? If you don't make my mom mad again," she added, the frankness of her look underscoring her words.

Ty smiled down at her as if he understood little girls all too well. "I will do my best to keep the peace." He flashed a smile up to Jessica as he squatted to Dovie's level. "And a shopping list is truly a wonderful thing."

Dovie grinned at him.

He grinned back, and Jessica was pretty sure the four-year-old was unabashedly smitten.

She, however, would accept the ride but dodge the attraction. Especially the attraction to a ruggedly handsome cowboy who might possibly be delivering an eviction notice to her in a matter of days.

Chapter Four

Vanilla and spice.

The scent hit Ty like a knock upside the head, because he hadn't ridden with a woman in the car for a long time. Sally Ann occasionally accompanied him into Council or McCall, but she liked floral scents, old-fashioned and a little heavy. And she was almost old enough to be his mother.

There was nothing heavy or old-fashioned about this scent. It wound around him like one of those sweet-smelling candles.

"I like riding in this car so much! We're way up high!"

Never was he so grateful for the prattle of a little kid, because he couldn't for the life of him think of things to say. *Awkward* didn't begin to cut it. "It's a great ride."

"Where are we headed?" Jessica asked.

"Council," he told her as he headed south on old 95. "That's where I'll take the car for repairs. This way you'll got a feel for it."

"If it's as small as Shepherd's Crossing, I don't think it will take all that long," she told him. "But it's good to get my bearings. It was dark when we came up this stretch on Wednesday."

"Where did you get the little hen? And the potatoes and peas?" he asked.

"We brought them with us," she told him. "Traveling on the day before Thanksgiving, every grocery store was full to the hilt. We didn't have time to wait in long lines, so I thought we'd make do. Rough it. And then we could shop on Friday. We had a marvelous chocolate stash that we designated for dessert," she added with a wink to her little girl.

"Mom loves chocolate a lot," Dovie assured him. "But then there were no stores so we didn't worry about it. And then the car wouldn't work so we had to worry about it 'cause we were out of stuff!"

"Pretty much," she agreed. "So thank you, again. Having your friend Sally stop by was a godsend. I don't know how everything will work out with the house, but I'm sure God's got His hand over us. He certainly has so far."

He wanted to tell her differently. To advise her that the God thing only went so far.

He didn't.

He closed his mouth and kept on driving.

"So this is Council," she said a few minutes later.

"This is it." He waited to hear that it wasn't big enough. Or pretty enough. Or populated enough. Instead, she smiled at him. "That was only twenty minutes."

He nodded. "Give or take."

"Twenty minutes is nothing," she declared as she climbed out of the Jeep. "In Nebraska, twenty minutes is considered next-door."

"That's where you ladies are from?" He studied her as they approached the store. "Except you don't sound Midwest. More like Mid-Atlantic."

"Originally from Pennsylvania. I lived there all my life, went to college, thought I knew it all and discovered I was wrong. At my mother's insistence I clung to my faith, then realized it was more for my good than hers. And it's got me— *us*—through some rough times."

"Christmas lights!" Dovie's excitement saved him the awkwardness of formulating a reply. "I love Christmas lights so much, Mommy!"

"I know you do, and we'll string ours up once we're settled. I think the first thing we need to do is invest in some new beds. And a solid kitchen table and chairs."

"And a Christmas tree." Dovie's sigh was the

embodiment of every small child during Advent. "And we can hang our specialest ormaments of all."

Jessica smiled at the butchered word. "We sure will."

She didn't look at him as if to challenge their right to dream. But that only made it worse, because unless the county admitted wrongdoing, how could she win? And counties rarely admitted fault in something like this.

"Can I ride in the cart?"

Jessica tipped a questioning smile down. "That will cut down our grocery room."

"How about this?" Ty picked Dovie up and sat her in a second cart. "Now Mom has room for groceries and you get a free ride. Pretty sweet."

"It is very sweet!" she exclaimed, grinning. "And look at how pretty this store is, Mommy! With so many things."

"It's a beautiful store," she agreed. "It's not huge by Pennsylvania standards, but it's just enough. No one needs too much, do they?"

She glanced up at him as she posed the question, and it was a question he'd asked a lot of folks over time. The irony of the question wasn't lost on him now. "Too much makes us think we never have quite enough." He kept his voice even. "The human tendency toward dissatisfaction."

"Always wanting more." She met his gaze

with a quiet look of agreement. "I've watched it ruin people. Families. Communities." She glanced around, approving. "This is perfect. Just enough."

"I don't even believe what I see!" Dovie slapped a hand to her forehead. "A little Christmas tree with all those itty-bitty glowing lights! Can we go closer, Mommy? Please?" The excitement in her voice made it a no-brainer. Who could say no to her? Not him. And when he moved the cart closer to the holiday display, Dovie clasped her hands together as if in prayer. "Isn't it the most perfect little bitty tree ever, Mommy?"

There were three of the little stoneware trees on display.

They weren't perfect.

Ty saw that right off.

Dovie didn't.

One of the local ladies ran a ceramics workshop and these were probably made right here in Council. The tiny colored plastic lights shimmered from the light bulb within and he glimpsed the reality then.

The simplicity of a child's eyes. The sweet joy of sparkle and light.

"Dovie, I love them!" exclaimed Jessica. "You have such a good eye for beautiful things!"

"I know." The girl blushed at the compliment. "I just love pretty things so much."

"Me, too."

And yet their clothing was simple. The car was simple. And the inherited house was the very definition of *simple*.

When they rolled past the little trees, Dovie swallowed hard. Then she smiled. "Maybe we can visit the little trees next week, when our car's better."

"I think we could." Jessica gave her a tender look of understanding. "It will give us something special to look forward to."

"It will!" Dovie clapped her hands in glee. She didn't beg for a tree. Many children would have.

Not her.

She grinned up at her mother, and when Jessica leaned across her cart to kiss the girl's cheek, Ty's heart pinched tight. So close…

He'd been so close to having what he'd always envisioned. It had been nestled in his hand, then snatched away.

"I smell cimmanon!"

"Cinn-a-mon," corrected her mother. But she smiled when she said it because it was impossible not to.

"I love it so much," added Dovie, and this time even her mother couldn't resist her imploring look.

"Sunday morning cinnamon rolls would be delightful," she agreed and headed for the small bakery. When she set a box of frosted cinnamon rolls in the cart basket, Dovie grinned.

"That will be so delicious, Mommy."

"I'm glad." She smiled at the girl, then finished shopping quickly.

Ty wanted to pay for the groceries.

She'd no doubt refuse and possibly be insulted. She said they were okay with money, but the urge to help had him reach for his wallet as they approached the checkout.

She stopped him with one soft, smooth hand on his. Her skin, so cool. Not pale, but not dark, either, like fresh honey right off the comb. "Don't even think it, cowboy."

"But—"

"While I appreciate the thought, Dovie and I have been making our own way for a while now. We're all right."

He left his wallet where it was, then wondered what *all right* meant, because if the car was as bad as he thought it was, that kind of repair bill could lay a family flat. At Christmas, no less.

Flat and homeless, you idiot.

"But I would love your help getting these bags back to your SUV," she told him. She swiped a debit card and entered a pin, and when the machine approved the purchase, she slipped the receipt into her purse. "The Lamberts live to eat again!" she proclaimed as they moved to the door.

Dovie laughed, then lifted her arms to him.

She needed help out of the cart. Of course.

He grasped her, then lifted as she wriggled her legs free of the seat. "Mommy says I'm getting too big for the seats, and I think I am because my legs don't even want to fit anymore." She giggled, and then she was in his arms, tucked against his chest. And when she slung her arms around his neck, old emotions threatened to drown him.

"I think this is a nice town, Mommy!" she called out as they followed Jessica across the parking lot. "Look at all those pretty flags!"

American flags flew proudly from several businesses lining Dartmouth Street.

"They're beautiful, honey."

And if Dovie hadn't won his heart before, she did when she brought up her tiny hand in a very proper salute.

Jessica paused. She sighed, then smiled. "Good form, kid."

"Thanks, Mommy."

"Shall I tuck her right in her seat?"

"Yes, please."

He settled Dovie in, then helped with the last few bags of groceries before putting the cart away. When he climbed into the car, he pointed diagonally. "There's a cute coffeehouse over there, but they're closed for winter."

"It's hard to keep things going when rough weather is a factor," Jess agreed. "But it gives us something to look forward to this spring."

"My mommy loves coffee shops," said Dovie.

"I love coffee," Jessica agreed. "But we'll make our own little coffee bar in the kitchen. And it will be sensational."

"I know we don't have much time with groceries on board, but let me give you a quick tour." He did a five-minute tour of the town, then gave them a view of the elementary school.

"I can go to that school when I'm five!" Dovie breathed the words as if awed. "And there will be lots of kids, Mommy!"

"There's only one class in each grade," Ty said.

"Just one?" Jessica didn't seem upset by that. In fact, she seemed pleased. "I went to a small school like that. I loved it. It was a real wake-up call to go to college where there were two thousand other freshmen. But I wouldn't change it." She smiled back at Dovie. "I'm in no hurry to pack you off to school, Dovie."

The step-by-step tasks of raising a child. Ty had wanted that. He'd wanted so much, none of it grandiose. Just normal. All he'd wanted was the

American dream. His wife. A family. A place to come home to.

"Ty, I don't see any Christmas tree sellers up here." She turned his way. "Where do people buy Christmas trees?"

"There is one, actually—we just didn't pass it. But a lot of folks buy a permit from the government and go into the forest and cut a tree."

"Cut it down? With a saw?" Dovie's eyes couldn't have gone wider.

"Exactly like that. Then you drag it out of the woods and tie it to a car or pop it into the bed of a pickup truck and bring it home."

"I can't even think of how much fun that would be!" She gasped the words as if the idea was more than she could bear. "To go in the forest and pick a tree just like Bear and his friends, Mommy! There might even be aminals in there!"

"Animals," she corrected her. "There could be, darling. Just like in your Bear books. But I don't think I've got the right tools. We might have to just buy one once the car is fixed."

"Then maybe next year we can go into a big forest."

"And that could be your kindergarten excursion tree, to mark your first year in school."

"For big schoolgirl Dovie!" Dovie smiled, smug.

"Yes."

Ty headed toward Shepherd's Crossing. When they reached the edge of town, he glanced at Jessica in time to see her brow draw down. "It's a little different. I know."

"Which is a shame, because it has potential," she told him. "The sweet houses, the quiet streets, the trees. Who wouldn't want to live in a town lined with all of these trees?"

He pulled into her driveway and parked behind her car. "I guess money got tight, jobs disappeared and things kind of dried up."

"Except the ranch you work on just bought several properties." She faced him over the hood of the SUV as she opened Dovie's door. "Who buys real estate in a dying town?"

"There are folks who want to bring things back to life. Restore things."

She looked surprised and happy to hear that. "Like the people who came to church this morning?"

"I expect." Suddenly he felt like he should explain why he hadn't come to church that morning. Or ever. He tamped down the temptation. "And others. It's pretty far gone, though."

"But filled with promise."

"Yeah?" He looked at her, then the town, as if in disbelief. "I'm not sure where you see that."

"All around us." She said the words softly, and for just a moment, he felt it. The promise she talked about. The hint of hope. Then his phone rang. It was Eric, probably wondering what he'd done about the squatters on the newly purchased property.

He let the call go to voice mail and helped bring groceries in. He'd explain things to Eric later. If it was as simple as reneging on the house, that would be one thing, but it was a middle house in a block of four. Losing it put serious limitations on whatever options Eric had in mind. Of course, things changed on a regular basis. That was life.

Once the groceries were inside, he moved to the door.

He didn't want to go. It was a silly reaction, but a part of him wanted to hang out. Play with Dovie. Watch Jessica put things away with quiet, decisive moves.

He started for the door. "Well, I've—"

Jessica had been pouring water into a coffee maker. She turned surprised. "You're not leaving before *cimmanon* rolls, are you?" She smiled, mispronouncing the name purposely.

"Well—"

"Oh, Mr. Ty, I think you should have *cimmanon* rolls and see my doll collection because they are the nicest little dollies in the whole world and they need people to look out for them. That's me," she told him, pointing at herself. "I think you can maybe stay for just a little while. Right?"

He wanted to.

But he didn't dare.

He knew the score. Knew it too well. A single mom, a winsome child, a home that needed work... Every aspect of the situation called to the nurturer in him, a side he'd let go of years ago.

He'd learned about risk and reward the hard way, which meant he wasn't willing to risk again. "I'd love to, but I have to get back to the ranch. I've got an afternoon date with about fourteen hundred head of cattle."

Dovie frowned.

"That's one thousand four hundred cows, Dovie."

"Over a thousand? I don't even know how to count to that many cows!" She planted her hands on her hips and stared up at him. "Mister, are you kidding me?"

Oh, his heart. He squatted low. "Would you like to come see the cows sometime this week?"

"I would love that so much!" She bounced into his arms and gave him a monster hug. "I'll dress so warm and I won't make big noises. Mommy says aminals do not like big noises so I'll creep around just like this." She released him and tiptoed around the small, shabby living room on the cutest sock-clad feet he'd ever seen.

"That's exactly how we walk around the cows," he fibbed. Then he grinned because he couldn't help himself. "Let's plan it around picking your car up, all right?" He raised his gaze to Jessica's and felt that pull again. The urge to stay. To help.

"Perfect. I've got several projects I'm working on—"

He frowned and arched a brow.

"I'm a graphic designer, so me and my laptop are a team," she told him. "I'm doing book covers for several authors, and magazine graphics for a couple of Western magazines. I'll work on those until we get the car situation worked out."

"I'll be by in the morning with the tow truck and get it down to Bud's Garage."

"And you're sure you won't stay?" she asked. She indicated the brewing coffee with a glance. "Coffee's about ready."

"Another time."

"Of course. Thank you, Ty." She moved forward to show him to the door and offered her hand. "You've helped make an awkward situation less so. I appreciate that—for both of us."

"My pleasure. Miss Dovie?"

Dovie skipped toward him, seized his hand

and made a good notch in his heart. "See you soon, Cowboy Ty!"

"I'm lookin' forward to it, little missy."

Her giggle followed him out the door, and as he crossed to his SUV, he surveyed the short street. Then the next one. And the one after that.

Less than a dozen streets made up the village part of Shepherd's Crossing. At least half the houses stood empty and a quarter of those needed extensive work.

He'd scoffed when Lizzie Fitzgerald began talking about revitalizing the town last summer. Then she'd married his friend Heath Caufield, and they had invited the entire town to the outdoor wedding.

And now people were getting together. Talking. Planning things.

He'd been ignoring it. He was good at ignoring things. He'd got good at letting life pass him by while he tended cows and calves and the occasional sheep that strayed his way from Pine Ridge, the Fitzgerald ranch that backed up to Carrington Acres.

Scanning his surroundings, he no longer wanted to ignore the needy town. He wanted to help polish it so when Dovie looked around, she saw something worth seeing.

Ridiculous.

They'd never make it here in Shepherd's

Crossing. The writing was on the wall. A struggle for the house, a struggle for existence, in a town already in the throes of disrepair.

Why would anyone do that by choice?

But as he drove away, he glanced down the empty Main Street, and for just a moment, he imagined it like Council. With flags waving. Flowerpots brimming. Twinkle lights on lampposts and wreaths on every door.

A silly dream. Foolish, really.

But for just a moment, he could see it. He didn't dare take a moment to believe it.

But he saw it, sure enough.

Chapter Five

Trapped.

By Tuesday afternoon, Jessica was going absolutely, positively stir-crazy. No car. No people. No noise.

Talk about too much of a good thing.

The internet worked, so they were able to watch some cute Christmas movies. She took Dovie for walks. They ventured into the woods across Route 95, but not too far because the last thing she wanted was to be a headline. Foolish Mother Takes Innocent Child into Dark, Snowy Woods. Never Heard from Again.

She missed Pennsylvania. She missed that feel of people all around, yet enough privacy to be truly rural. She missed—

Her ringing phone interrupted her pity party, and Ty's name lit up her screen. "Hello, this is Jessica."

"It's Ty. Bud just called and he'll have the car ready by early afternoon tomorrow. Can I swing by and pick you gals up first thing, give Dovie a tour of the cows, and then we'll head down to Council and grab the car?"

"Yes. Yes. A thousand times yes," she told him.

"Are you all right?"

"I find that I'm not used to being locked in a tiny place with no company, no nearby shopping or anything resembling normal life. I've discovered that I am neither reclusive nor do I have hermit tendencies, because right now I'm missing people so much that I can't even describe my emotions at hearing your voice."

He burst out laughing and it sounded nice to hear him laugh. "That's so funny."

"We are not amused." She told him that in her prissiest British accent, stolen from a few of her favorite shows. "But we will dress warmly and come meet the Carrington cows."

"I'll come by at nine."

"Perfect."

She set out clothing that night so they wouldn't have to rush in the morning. Dovie didn't like to rush. She liked to think about things, including her clothing, and changing outfits three or four times wasn't unusual for her.

Gloves. Hats. Scarves. She put a folded set

of unicorn thermals on the top, hoping Dovie wouldn't fight her on the layers. Layers were a given, but there hadn't been much playing outside last year, with the bitter cold and harsh winds.

Already it was different here.

The trees, the hills, the mountains, the rolling plateau teeming with ranch life.

Ty pulled into the driveway the next morning as promised, and when Dovie spotted his SUV, she began getting dressed.

Jessica opened the door and welcomed him in. "We're being held up by a very small diva who has to get her look just right to see the cows in all their bovine glory."

He laughed softly. "And me, I just layer up whatever I find, and figure the cows can't tell buffalo plaid from Carhartt blue. We should get her some bib overalls," he went on as Dovie tugged on a pair of fleecy warm-up pants over her leggings. "They're the thing up here for being outside. I expect she'd like to go sledding. Don't you think?" He turned those big blue eyes her way.

Whoa.

Dangerous weapon. And he'd shaved the stubble he'd sported before.

Eyes as blue as a midsummer sky, and filled

with trust and warmth. But something else, too. Some hint of sadness.

She recognized that look. She'd lived it the past two years, but grief and children made poor housemates. Dovie deserved joy. Light. Faith. Goodness. And she'd made the move to ensure every bit of that.

"I'm ready!"

Lopsided ponytails peeked out from beneath a fuzzy hat, above a puffy jacket. "I don't think I really need so many pants, Mommy." She crossed the room to them, stuck out one leg and frowned. "I don't think the cows wear so many pants. Do they?" She peered up at Ty, but Jessica saved him from answering.

"Cows are farm animals. We are not. And if you want to see them, you need to mind your mother. Got it?"

Dovie sighed. "Got it. But it's not very comfortable."

Ty held the door open and Dovie crossed to the SUV. He turned to Jessica as she locked the door. "I didn't think she ever complained."

"Oh, we have our moments," Jessica told him, but then she smiled Dovie's way. "But she's got a gentle nature. Inquisitive and caring. I'm a little more argumentative, so I'm trying to learn to be more easygoing. Like Dovie."

"Being a single mom doesn't allow a whole lot

of latitude, I imagine," he said as they crossed to the car, and to her surprise, he paused on her side and opened her door for her.

Jessica couldn't remember the last time a man had done that for her. It felt wonderful, as if going to visit the cows was a date.

It wasn't, of course.

But Dovie's excitement and the clear, bright Idaho day seemed made for adventure. When Ty turned down a long lane that wound up at a sprawling cattle ranch, she gave his arm a poke. "This huge place is the ranch?"

"Yes." He followed the direction of her gaze and made a face. "Pretty impressive, huh?"

"Stunning. I brought my camera along. Do you mind if I take a few pictures?"

"A few years ago we would have shunned the idea, but then Google came along, privacy disappeared and shots of the ranch are everywhere. Shoot away."

"So the Carringtons are a private sort?" She climbed out of the front seat while he opened Dovie's door on that side of the car.

He hesitated before he nodded. "It's a good place to live if you're searching for quiet."

"Ty, you've brought your new friends!" Sally Ann waved from a side door. "When you're done visiting the cattle, come back to the house for breakfast."

"Will do. Gals, we're going to shift into a different vehicle to go uphill." He'd unfastened Dovie's seat from the back of his SUV and secured it in the back of a more rugged utility vehicle.

"Are there baby cows?" Dovie asked, and she frowned when Ty shook his head.

"Not now, but in two months there will be. Then Mommy can bring you over and we'll show you baby cows everywhere."

"Like a gazillion?"

"Like a thousand, so it will seem like a gazillion." He drove up the farm lane and parked. "We won't go through gates today, but this will give you a taste of country."

"It's so fun to see so many big cows!" Dovie breathed. "Can you lift me up high? Please?"

"Gladly." He raised her up, then turned to block the wind from her pixie face. "What do you think?"

"I like the red-and-white ones the best because they have curly hair."

"Those are Herefords or Hereford crosses," he told her. "They have curly heads."

"I have always wanted curly hair, from when I was so small," she told him.

"That's a long time," he teased. "But I think your hair is real pretty, Dovie. With or without curls."

"Thank you." She preened up at him, then

turned her attention back to the cows. "Don't they get, like, so freezing out here?"

"Animals have lived outside from the time God created them," Jessica reminded her. "They grow thick fur coats to help them stay warm."

"And they'll come around the side of the barn with the least wind sometimes," Ty told her. "The barn blocks the wind."

"But what if it's a really, really big snow?" she wondered, clearly worried. "Do you help them, Mr. Ty?"

"I sure do. There's a bunch of us who help them, Dovie."

"Oh, good." She leaned her cheek against his in a charming gesture. "It's good for us to take care of aminals. And people, too."

He didn't move his cheek from hers.

He stood still, watching the big cows munch sweet green hay with Dovie in his arms. Jessica captured it quietly on camera before he turned. "That wind's sharp, kiddo. Let's check out the barn and say hi to the horses. And there are half a dozen pigs in a pen out back."

"You raise pigs to sell, too?" asked Jessica.

He sent a cautionary look toward Dovie. "Not exactly."

Jessica laughed. "Dovie knows where meat comes from. The more we know, the better prepared we are for life."

They stopped by the pig enclosure and six porkers waddled over, grumping and snorting.

Ty stood Dovie on the low rail and handed her apple slices. "See what they think of these."

"Oh! Their faces are gunky and so slippery!" Dovie drew back her hand, casually swiped it along her fleece pants, then reached for more apples to feed her new friends. "Why are their faces so wet?"

"I have no idea, but they sure seem to like those apples," he told her.

"I like apples, too. They're one of my favorite things. Are there baby animals in here?" She posed the question hopefully, gazing up at him.

He shook his head. "Too cold in December and January. Baby animals come closer to spring. But the ranch next door has some baby sheep," he added. "They have lambs all year now. Would you like to visit them sometime?"

"I would love to see a baby lamb!" She gave a convincing sheep imitation. "I can practice talking to them, just like that."

He carried her over to visit the stabled horses, then back around to the car.

"This is a very big farm." She faced him straight on, her little face close to his. "How does somebody get such a very big farm?"

"Mostly they spend a lot of money and do a lot of work," he told her, then he tweaked one ponytail as he settled her into the back seat. "You ready for breakfast?"

She bobbed her head. "So ready! I was too 'cited to eat this morning, because we were going to have so much fun, but now I'm so 'cited to eat! Isn't that funny, Mr. Ty?"

"It is funny." He watched as she fastened her seat belt, then smiled. "And adorable. You're pretty cute, kid."

"So are you!" She grinned up at him. "And I got to see so many cool an-i-mals." She stretched the syllables to get the proper order. "So thank you! It was, like, the best farm trip ever!"

Chapter Six

Her words. Her enthusiasm. Her joy…

The combination softened the rusty locks on his heart. He'd tucked himself away years ago, and you couldn't get much further away than a wide-ranged ranch in western Idaho. But this past summer, with the hint of new hope coming to the neighboring farms. To the town…

Something was awakening in him. Something he'd put to sleep a long time ago.

"Now, you folks come and eat—there's a lot of good food here," instructed Sally Ann. "I made hash brown rounds, a farm favorite," she told them. "And I was thinking about you two when I was up in McCall with my dad," she went on as they filled their plates from the warming trays on the counter. "Dad won't be going back to his house, and he had three boxes of Christmas decorations he'll never use again, so I brought them

back here to give to you. I figured any house
with a little one would love to decorate properly
for Christmas."

"I love Christmas so much." Dovie scrambled
into a tall chair with help from Ty and inhaled
deeply. "This smells so good, Miss Sally! I think
we need to have so many pretty lights at Christ-
mastime, don't you?"

"So Santa can find his way to your chimney?"
asked Ty with a smile.

Dovie shook her head. "No. To show baby
Jesus how much we love Him and that we want
to have a pretty party, just for Him. For His
happy birthday, mister. We don't want Him
to think we forgot His most special day ever.
Right?"

His birthday.

Ty's heart slowed.

Why had he thought that an extraordinary
child would give an ordinary answer?

"The best reason for the season is that sweet
baby," added Jessica. She smiled at Dovie. "And
I'd love to go through those decorations, Miss
Sally."

"Just call me Sally," she told her. "I'm happy
to find a home for them, and Dad will feel the
same way. He's ready to be done living on his
own," she explained. "My kids are grown and
only one lives in the area, so Dad and I are going

to buy one of the village homes and fix it up. That way we're close to my work, close to church and close to the village businesses. When we have some again. So we'll be living near you gals." She beamed a hearty smile their way.

Jessica waved a piece of Texas-style toast. "Do you think it's doable? To bring life back to the town? Because compared to Council, it's barely breathing."

"Overdue but doable. Yes." Sally poured a mug of coffee and slipped onto a nearby stool. "It's amazing what folks can do when they all work together. We just kind of forgot that for a while."

"May I have some more syrup, please?" Dovie asked.

"You sure can, sweetie. Does my heart good to see a child like real maple syrup."

"I got spoiled growing up in Pennsylvania," noted Jessica. "We had real maple syrup all the time. There were small farms producing it every year. When I moved here, I had to have it shipped in at first. Then one of the big-box stores began carrying it from Canada and it was like a taste of home."

"What brought you west?" The minute Ty asked the question, he realized his mistake.

She didn't look up. She gazed down, at her food. Her hands didn't move. Neither did her head. Then she drew in a deep breath and faced him. "I met Dovie's father in college. He was Lakota, I was part Onondaga and we belonged to a Native American social justice group. He challenged me to reacquaint myself with my Native American roots. To gain a greater understanding of life on both sides of the reservation."

Sally made a small sound. She didn't say anything, but she moved to put her coffee mug in the sink.

"Then they got married and my mom moved with my dad, and then my grandma died and I never even really met her. Not once." Regret darkened Dovie's normally happy tone.

"I'm sorry." Ty aimed a look of apology to Jessica. "I didn't mean to pry."

"You didn't. Not really. I don't keep secrets from Dovie—most of the time." She hiked her brows, gently teasing her daughter. "We learned a great deal about our history on both sides of the ocean because I'm a true melting pot. But after Dovie's father passed away, I wanted Dovie to grow up in a kindly town. Childhood passes all too quickly," she added with a smile. "A few years of fairyland aren't too much to ask."

"I couldn't agree more," said Sally. She motioned to the clock as she drew her jacket down from a hook. "I'm riding over to check on Dad for an hour or so, then I'm meeting Lizzie Caufield and the crew at Pine Ridge to help plan the Christmas potluck we've got scheduled for Christmas Eve. Why don't you come by Pine Ridge Ranch around three thirty?"

"I couldn't barge in," Jessica protested. "That would be rude."

"It would be wonderful," Sally Ann corrected her. "We can use all hands on deck, and what better way to show your little one how a town works together than by jumping in and helping out?"

"You'll have your car back by then," Ty said. "And I expect Dovie would like to meet those lambs."

"Oh, that's right! Is that the farm you told me about, mister? Because I would love to see those babies!"

"Seems like I'm outnumbered." Jessica looked from Ty to Dovie and back again. "Yes, we'll be there. You're right. There's no way to get to know a town better than by volunteering. And Lizzie asked us to come by."

"I'll text Lizzie and the gals and let them know. It will be a good planning session. It's so nice to see this town planning things again," Sally added. "We've been in a dry spell, but the drought is over. Rain falls soft upon our fields."

Sally didn't mean the literal rain.

She meant the promise of hope and the strength of faith from the old Celtic prayer.

Ty was totally on board with the hope thing. The faith mandate?

Not so much.

But when he caught little Dovie whispering a quiet prayer over her fruit-glazed pancakes, it was like looking into a mirror. Back when he was innocent. Believing. Trusting.

Then he'd grown up. And found out the hard way that faith didn't move mountains and a broken heart could still be broken nearly five years down a long, lonely road.

"I'm so glad you invited us over to do this." Jessica's voice drew him out of the past and into the present. "Seeing the animals. Seeing a big farm or ranch like this, whatever you call it. It's marvelous. It brings back so many good memories for me."

"I'm glad."

"I'll see you later," said Sally as she withdrew keys from a hooked rack near the door. "I'm taking the ranch SUV, Ty, so I can move more things today."

He stood quickly. "Sally, I can help you."

"No need. I'm just killing time while we finish things up at the hospital and Dad's place. The new folks want to be in before Christmas so if I bring down a load each day, it'll be done in a week or two. See you gals later!" she called over her shoulder as she hurried out the door.

"Does she put up all your Christmas decorations, mister?"

"Mr. Ty," said Jessica.

Ty shrugged. "I think the *mister* thing is kind of cute," he told Dovie, then he waggled his brows. "But that might be because the kid saying it is supercute."

"Thank you!" She sat up straighter and brightened her smile. "But will Miss Sally put up your Christmas decorations, because a big house like this must have a lot of decorations, right? So you can be bright and shiny?"

The ranch hadn't been bright or shiny in a long time.

He was unsure of what to say, but Jessica saved him.

"I bet they work together on it once they're not busy with cows, but you saw how many cows there are, right?"

Dovie bobbed her head and spread her arms. "So many!"

"And that takes a lot of love and a lot of work for Ty and all the cowboys here on the ranch."

"And the pigs and horses."

"Them, too. So I think we'll give Ty and Sally some time to get things done. Okay? We don't want folks to think we're hurrying them."

"Okay, Mom. I won't even hardly say anything about it."

"Perfect." Jessica slid off her stool and carried her dish to the sink. "And now we're going to take ten minutes and surprise Sally with a clean kitchen when she gets back."

"I can do this," said Ty, but Jessica made a face at him.

"I know you can, but it's nice for folks to work together. And it teaches young ones how to get on in this world. Acts of kindness are never out of style."

The way she talked stirred him. Her gentle thoughts moved him. And the way she looked in those black leggings and rose-and-pink shirt was an absolute pleasure of a different sort.

He smiled as he rinsed the dishes and set them into the dishwasher.

She had beauty and strength. Something that went above and beyond the norm. When they had the dishes put up, they drove to Council. Within an hour he was saying goodbye and realized that was the last thing he wanted to do.

"Ty, thank you for all of your help." She'd paid the car bill and hadn't winced. The total bill had been just shy of a thousand dollars, and he couldn't believe that wasn't a hit on her budget.

Still, she'd paid it and hadn't complained.

"Glad to do it. And if there's anything you need, just let me know."

"My house?" she said brightly, then laughed when he looked chagrined.

"Listen, we'll get that straightened out," he promised. "If it's really your house, we'll renege on the deal. It's not like we paid a fortune for it. We didn't. So let's just settle that now. I'll have the paperwork drawn up so that everything is signed over to you."

"Ty." She reached out and took his hands in hers, and suddenly he didn't care that the wind had picked up or that the snow was now falling with a ferocity he hadn't seen yet this season. "If the county messed up, the county should fix it. That's not your fault. Or mine. And if they had taxes due, they had my address as owner of record. Let me have a face-off with them. Then we'll see."

"I can go with you."

She shook her head. "No need. Dovie and I like to take things on. I want her to know that women can do anything they need to do to take care of themselves."

"Women power."

"Women empowerment," she corrected him. "I don't need more power than a man. But I need to be respected for my own self-worth."

There had to be a reason she said it that way,

but now wasn't the time to push. "Have a safe drive home."

"We will! Thank you, mister!"

He couldn't help it.

He grinned.

Something about that cute kid calling him "mister" and grinning up at him. Trusting him to hold her. Carry her.

His clunky old heart stretched inside his chest as he watched her pull away.

He'd have to call Eric about the house, but the simple fact was that neither brother needed the house in town and they could buy another block of houses without a blink of an eye, which meant Jessica had a whole lot more to lose than the Carrington brothers.

Chapter Seven

He called his brother as he walked toward the market, just in case they still had those little ceramic Christmas trees. Eric answered as he approached the door. "Hey, what's up? You never call. You okay?"

"Fine, everything's good. That snag I told you about, the woman who thinks the house on Harrison Street is hers? I'm backing off the claim. We're going to let her have it, regardless of what went wrong."

"We're what? We're giving away a house? Ty. Stop. Think. Look around. Have you hit your head? Are you in a hospital? Because normal-thinking people don't go around giving away houses. What's up with you and this woman?"

"Nothing." The minute he said it, he realized it wasn't true, because there was something. He wasn't sure what, but it was there in her smile.

Her walk. Her voice. "She inherited the house. Sent in the required paperwork. Somewhere the county dropped the ball and never sent her a tax bill."

"So she thought she could have it tax-free for two years?" Eric sounded doubtful. Real doubtful. But then he laughed. "Okay, you're in charge. Do whatever you think is best. I figure if we end up with a few extra properties in town that don't sell or don't appreciate, at least we tried to be part of it all. Not like it's going to make a difference," he went on, and the doubt in his voice came through loud and clear. "We've owned that ranch for thirteen years and not once has anyone lifted a finger to help anyone else."

"Things are changing."

"We'll see." Eric's voice shifted as he changed the subject. "Dad wants to know if you're heading east for Christmas. Mom will be sad if you don't, but she said I shouldn't bother you about it because the holidays are hard for you."

"Mom's right, so why are you bothering me about it?" His mother had the biggest heart known to mankind. A rich woman who walked around like everyday normal. She had nothing of her husband's exaggerated love for success and had set a solid example for her three sons from the time they were old enough to walk.

"Because they're not exactly young," Eric reminded him. "Dad's going to be sixty-five next spring and Mom's only a year younger. What if something horrible happens and we lose Mom or Dad? And then you look back and realize the times you missed. It wouldn't hurt you to spend a few days with them."

Eric was right.

He hated that. Mostly because it was his big brother and big brothers loved to be right, but also because he knew better. He used to counsel people about this very thing, until—

"Tell Mom I'll call her. We'll set up a plan."

"And I don't have to punch you?"

"I didn't say that," he shot back, then he laughed. It was a rusty laugh, but for that moment he felt like laughing. "You're right. We'll figure out the time frame so we're not dumping all the ranch work on the men and Sally."

"I'll call you soon."

"Okay." He hung up the phone, surprised. The conversation had taken a distinct turn toward the unexpected. He'd been fighting off family parties and joyous occasions for years.

Now it didn't seem quite as harsh. It seemed almost normal to be thinking about his mom and dad. Getting together for the holidays.

He walked into the store and crossed to the Christmas display. Two of the little trees had been sold, but the third one remained.

He brought it up front.

The cashier found a box, and he smiled as he carried the box to the cab of the pickup.

Dovie would love it.

She would smile and clap her hands, and the thought of her joy made him happy.

What was happening to him? How come all of a sudden he was turning back into a real person with a range of feelings and emotions?

Maybe it's not so sudden. Maybe it's been a long time coming.

The mental nudge made him pause.

Then he shoved the idea aside.

He used to believe in God's timing. God's strength. God's omniscience, His importance.

He'd stopped seeing God as an important entity when he'd held his wife's dying body in his arms on a cold, wet night on a rain-slicked New Jersey road.

The wind whipped his face.

It had whipped his face that night, too. With rain, not snow. But slick leaves had reduced traction and when he'd swerved the wheel to avoid hitting a child, a little boy that had run into the road after a ball…

The car had spun a full arc, then hurled itself into a tree. And Lisbeth was gone. Just like that. Her and their unborn daughter. Both gone. And he'd been alone ever since.

He opened the truck door and set the package inside.

He hadn't bought a Christmas present for anyone in a long time.

Buying this one felt good. The thought of Dovie's smiling face felt more than good. It felt as if he was on the verge of something so special and wonderful that it couldn't be contained.

He climbed into the truck and started the engine. And then he breathed.

For years he'd felt like he was holding his breath. Waiting for more tragedy. More sorrow. Wanting to hurt back the way he was hurting. He'd been full of anger and remorse. What if he'd driven slower? What if he'd stopped by the store first, the way Lisbeth wanted? But he hadn't done either of those things, and then she was gone. It was too late.

He backed out of the parking spot.

Dovie wanted a Christmas tree adventure. He called Sally on his cell phone and asked her to run an errand for him.

"Sure, glad to. What do you need?" she asked.

"Christmas tree permits. From the forest office up there in McCall."

"How many do you need?"

"Two," he said. "No, make it three. That way we have an extra if we need it. There's always someone that can use a Christmas tree, right?"

"Yes. Of course." If his request surprised her, she didn't let it show. "I'll grab three permits and put them on the ranch debit card."

"Perfect. How's your dad doing, Sally?"

"Tired. So tired. But he's hanging in there, Ty, and if EJC Pharmaceuticals can come up with some sort of immunotherapy anticancer drug and kick this disease to the curb, I'm going to be one happy person."

"You know they're working on it." His parents had poured millions of dollars into a new facility bordering the University of Pennsylvania in their strident attack to unlock anticancer codes. They were close, but not there yet. "Right now I wish we had all the kinks worked out."

"I know. It's just hard, seeing Dad go through this. But he's being strong so there's no reason for me to whine about it. I'll see you later. With the permits."

"Thank you, Sally."

He hung up as he headed north to the ranch. He'd been born to money. Born to brilliance. Born to a sympathetic nature that loved people. Helping them. Guiding them.

Eric had got their father's sense of science.

He'd got their mother's empathetic heart.

And Brent, Ty's younger brother, was a maverick, determined to go his own way. The Carrington prodigal.

And at the heart of their business was a possible cure for cancer. So much hope and promise lingered almost within reach, but problems two years ago had slowed down the research studies. Not all patients could tolerate the new treatments, which meant they either thrived and emerged cancer-free...

Or they died. And no one was quite sure why. But from that reality lawsuits and money-hungry attorneys had emerged.

He pulled into the barnyard as a text came through from Heath Caufield. Look familiar? A photo of six Angus/Hereford crosses stared back at him, chewing their cud as if they belonged on that side of the Fitzgerald fence.

He texted back quickly. Did they push through?

The reply was quick. Yup.

He should have checked for snowdrifts earlier. Or had George check. If snow piled up around the live electric wire, it pulled the charge into the ground. Cows might be placid, but they weren't stupid. They would nudge one cow into the fence. If the cow didn't react, then the other cows knew the fence wasn't charged and would push through. Be right there.

He added layers of clothes and met George. Then they headed across fields to where Pine Ridge Ranch edged up to Carrington Acres.

George and Heath led the cows back through the opening while Ty restrung the fence. Then they shoveled the snow away from the knoll before installing a short length of flexible snow fencing. "Hopefully this will redirect the snow away from the electric fence."

"Until the sheep knock it over. But we won't have them in this pasture for a good eight weeks," Heath told Ty. "It buys you time. Why don't you two come up to the house for coffee and food? Corrie made her famous Irish stew and biscuits. And since Sally's here planning food for the Christmas thing, you might as well eat here." He indicated the Carrington ranch with a jut of his chin. "Because unless one of you two is cooking, your stove's mighty cold about now."

"It sounds good," said George. "I won't say no."

Ty agreed. "Me, either." They climbed back into the utility vehicle and followed Heath across the upper pasture, then a lower one that led to the Pine Ridge sheep barns. And there, parked next to the Carrington Acres SUV, was Jessica's car.

"The women have taken over the front room," advised Heath as he led the way through the back entry, closest to the kitchen. "But Cookie and Corrie will take pity on us."

"'Long as those boots come off." Bob, aka

Cookie, Cook frowned from the kitchen. "Floor's warm and there's plenty of food."

"It smells amazing," noted Ty. He set his hat and jacket on a hook and went to wash his hands.

A flurry of little feet headed their way as Zeke and Dovie skidded to a stop along the long, tiled hall. "I told you it was my friend!" Dovie launched herself into his arms as if she belonged there. "Hey, Mr. Ty! My mom and Zeke's mom and some other people and Miss Sally are all doing stuff out there!" She pointed toward the living room. "Come see!"

"Dovie." Jessica appeared in the hallway looking just as pretty and unruffled as she had a few hours ago. Did that mean things had gone fine at the county office building? "I think Ty and his friend came in to get something to eat." She reached out for Dovie as if embarrassed. "You can't go jumping on people, honey. It just isn't done."

"Except it's pretty nice to get a welcome like that," Ty told her. "I'd say any man that got a welcome like that on a regular basis is pretty well-off. Wouldn't you?"

Chapter Eight

Oh, her heart. Gazing up into Ty's eyes, seeing the warmth there. Seeing the way he held Dovie, the way he talked to her, the way he seemed to care about things.

Heat climbed her neck, onto her cheeks. "I expect most good men would love a warm welcome," she agreed. "But manners are important, too."

He grinned at her as he handed Dovie over, and she wasn't sure if her heart sped up or just skipped a dozen beats. Whatever it did felt right. And not so right. Ty and his family had a lot of clout in this town, and she hadn't come to Idaho for romance. She'd messed that up once already. Once was enough. But she'd got Dovie out of the deal, and she wouldn't trade her beloved daughter for anything.

She herded Dovie back to the living room.

Lizzie looked up. "Dovie's got good taste in friends, I'd say."

Jessica's complexion was dark enough to fight off an obvious blush, but when Lizzie smirked, the blush won. "We're thrilled to be meeting so many nice people here now," Jessica told her, and she stressed the *so many* purposely. "It's pretty lonely in town."

"But not for long, we hope." Sally patted Jessica's knee when she sat down. "With some hope, we will make a difference and how nice to have you and Dovie as part of that difference."

"Well, that's the thing." Jessica made a face. "The county is insisting that I don't own the house."

"What?" Melonie sat more forward, surprised.

"What do you mean?" asked Lizzie. "Who told you that?"

"The county tax receiver when I was down at their offices a short while ago. I inherited the property, filled out the paperwork and sent it back, and thought it was all set. But I never got a tax bill. I never thought to follow up on it, but now here I am, in my house, but it's not my house anymore. They sold it to Ty's family for back taxes just a few weeks ago. Deal's done. Game over."

The women were all staring at her as if this

wasn't possible, but Jessica knew it was not only possible… it was reality.

"So do we have to move, Mommy? Because I don't want to move again, and I want to love our house." Dovie came closer and leaned against her mother. "'Member you said it was a old house, but it just needed someone to love it? Just like people? Well, I love it, Mommy. I love it so much and now we've got all our pretty Christmas things to put up. If we don't do it, the house might be so sad."

Oh, man.

She shouldn't have spoken so frankly in front of her smart daughter because Dovie caught on way too quick. "We'll see how it goes, honey."

"Sure will." Lizzie whistled lightly, and when Heath poked his head around the corner, she motioned toward the kitchen. "Can you ask Ty to come out here please, darling?"

Heath stared at her, then exchanged looks with several of the women. "When she whistles like she's calling a horse, I know someone's in big, big trouble. I'm just glad it's not me this time."

"Funny." She held his gaze and he backed up, hands up in surrender.

"Ty. You're wanted in the living room," Heath called over his shoulder. "And I've seen firing squads that look more friendly." He winked at the group. "I don't know what you've done, but—" he patted Ty's shoulder as Ty came down the tiled hall "—I'll be prayin' for you."

Ty paused near Heath and faced the seated women. "Am I in trouble because the cows got out? Did they eat someone's Christmas wreath? Did they knock down a fence? I'll take care of it. I promise." He glanced around and when his gaze landed on Jessica and Dovie, he paused. "You all right, Jessica?"

"She is not all right, because you and your brother bought her house and she can't keep it," said Lizzie. Jessica couldn't help but admire her tough-girl tone. "So if we want Jessica to stay in Shepherd's Crossing, she needs this fixed. Which comes back to you."

"You went to the county and they didn't admit their mistake?" He faced Jessica more fully. "Really?"

"They not only didn't acknowledge their mistake, they said they had no record of my paperwork being filed, hence no address for me, and no tax bill sent to me. Which means they're off the hook because in their eyes, your ranch owns the house fair and square."

He looked at her, then Dovie. Then he shrugged lightly, and when he did that, she was so very tempted to kick him in the shins that her foot twitched.

"Dovie." He bent low and held the little girl's

gaze. "Do you want to stay in Shepherd's Crossing with your mom?"

"I do!" She bobbed her head fervently. "And do pretty Christmas things and make it so special for baby Jesus's birthday. My mom wants to do that, too," she assured him, with such an earnest look that all the women smiled.

All the women except her, because Jessica was still contemplating kicking Ty for getting Dovie's hopes up.

Fair was fair. She'd never followed up on the paperwork, so this could be her fault. She hated that, but she was willing to admit it.

"Then I'll fix it tomorrow," he promised. He raised his gaze to Jessica and she didn't want her heart to melt…but it did. "I'll sign the property over to you and we'll get everything notarized the way it should be."

Sign it over to her?

Just like that?

Quick tears came to her eyes because she'd spent the last four years pretty much at war with everything around her. This had seemed like one more in a long list of ongoing battles, so to have it not become a battle was a huge relief. "You can't be serious."

"I'm almost always serious," he told her.

"Sad, but true," said Heath from the hallway, but he was grinning.

"So I'm serious about this, too," Ty continued. "Dovie needs a house. You need a house. I already have a house." He smiled and gave Dovie's head a light noogie. "So why do I need another one?"

"Because you bought it for investment," she told him. "Do you mean it, Ty?" She wanted him to read her gaze, to understand the depth of his words because it wasn't just a promise to her. She'd been dealing with broken promises from the time she said "I do" at a natural stone altar nearly six years ago. This was a promise to Dovie. "This isn't a casual conversation we're having here." She dipped her chin toward her daughter, standing between them.

"Deal's done, ma'am." He said it in cowboy lingo, and if she could paint an image of a classic cowboy, wooing a fair maid, it was Ty Carrington, on his knees, chatting with her and Dovie. "I called my brother this afternoon and let him know we needed to release the property either way. He's a jerk sometimes, but he was totally on board with this. We'll sign things over tomorrow."

"I knew you'd help us!" Dovie leaped onto him again and gave him a big hug. "I just knew it, mister! I told my mommy not to cry because we'd get this all fixed up. Right?" She beamed up at him, then down at Jessica.

"You cried?" His voice…the look of concern…the empathy in his gaze as he posed the question put her heart right back into overdrive.

"Not for long, because we're strong women," she answered, choking back emotion again because she wasn't accustomed to people being nice to her. "But there may have been a tear or two, more from anger than anything else because I didn't follow through when I should have. So it was self-directed fury. Nothing else."

"'Cept the rug," Dovie told him, and she flashed a look of sincerity to him, then her mother. "Right, Mommy?"

"The rug?" Ty looked puzzled, and once again Jessica realized she shouldn't say anything in front of her chatterbox daughter. "What rug?"

"Just an offhand comment about having it pulled out from under me," she muttered, wishing she could crawl into a hole.

"'Cause she's so stinkin' tired of having that happen," Dovie declared. She grinned, as if delighted that she'd remembered the phrasing so perfectly. "Right, Mommy?"

"And on that note, I think we should pause and eat because I expect Jessica could use a break from total public humiliation about now. I want to thank you, Ty." Lizzie crossed the room and hugged him.

He seemed awkward, as if he wasn't used to hugs. Or gatherings. Or being the center of attention.

"I'm beyond grateful to you, because once we get past Christmas, I want to work with Jessica to get our little town newsletter off the ground, and who better to help me than our own resident graphic designer?" She poked his arm gently as she went by. "Well done."

"Food smells marvelous," agreed Sally. "Corrie, if you'd share your secret to that Irish stew, I'd be grateful and so would the entire Carrington ranch, I suspect."

"A lot of Worcestershire sauce and onion, and if you throw a dash of red-hot sauce in, now you've got a real warms-you-up-from-within pot of stew."

"And Angus beef," Ty added.

"The best around," agreed Corrie. She smiled at him and took Dovie by the hand. "I'll fix a plate of food for Zeke and Dovie, if that's all right. If we can eat while the twins and baby Jo Jo are napping, then we can have unfettered baby time when we're done."

"And the potluck Christmas party is all planned," said Melonie. She stood and stretched. "Ty, Sally offered up smoked beef for the feast. I think that's going to fall on your holiday to-do list."

"I didn't used to have a holiday to-do list," he told her. "Now all of a sudden a bunch of women come to town and there are to-do lists everywhere."

He frowned at Melonie, which made her laugh, and when she'd moved to the kitchen, he turned back to Jessica. "I didn't mean to embarrass you. Sorry."

"I did that all on my own by getting emotional," she assured him. "And saying too much in front of my daughter."

"Well, I did kind of embarrass you." His gentle expression indicated he wasn't going to let her take the blame. "But I've gotta say, you're real pretty when you get all shy and funny like that."

"I am not shy. Nor funny."

He made a face of doubt, then acquiesced in such a nice way that she wondered what life would be like being teased by this man for, oh, say…forever? Clearly the whole house thing had her overcome with emotions, because the thought of romance and happily-ever-afters had gone out of her vocabulary years before. "We'll just leave it at pretty, then."

She sighed softly, then smiled. "Thank you."

"You're welcome. I think my food's gone cold."

"Oh, no." Her mouth dropped open in surprise. "I can't believe I didn't think of that. Oh, Ty, I'm sorry."

"Well, this big fancy ranch has a microwave, so I think it's all right."

He stepped back and motioned to the kitchen. "After you, ma'am."

Oh, that cowboy code. His gentleness. His manners. Yes, she saw the shadows in his eyes. Sensed a sadness in him. She used to dream of a kind, gentle, loving man.

Silly schoolgirl dreams, of course.

Yet when Ty was around, those old thoughts came back to life.

She needed to put them to rest. She couldn't risk a broken heart to mess up her start in a new town, especially if the house was truly hers now. With the house, she and Dovie could live here affordably.

And when she sat down at the Caufield/ Fitzgerald table with a bowl of stew and freshly baked bread, surrounded by a good, kind mix of people...

For the first time in over five years, Jessica Lambert felt like she'd finally come to a place she could call home.

Chapter Nine

"I have changed our plans," Mary Clare Carrington announced when Ty answered the phone the next morning. "Instead of you coming to New Jersey, we're all coming west for the holidays. I've been wanting to do a big Western Christmas the past few years, but Dad was too busy. This year I put my foot down. We're arriving on the twenty-third and staying through New Year's."

"Dad never takes off a week for Christmas," said Ty, because according to his father, time off was time wasted not curing disease or offering pain relief. "What can I do to help get ready?" he went on. "Does Sally know?"

"I just spoke to her," answered his mother. "She and I are going to work out a menu that's totally Western and full-on barbecue tradition, but she told me the little church in town closed.

That's such a shame." Genuine remorse deepened her tone. "We'll have to drive to Council for services, but that will be fine. I'm so excited about all of this, Tyler. Christmas together."

The thought that they were heading west for Christmas seemed right this year. "Well, the folks in town have been doing their own services at the church. Nothing major. But nice. I guess."

"I love resourceful people."

Ty knew the truth in that.

"Then we'll do church service right there, with the rest of the town."

He ignored that deftly. "Let me know what I can do to help get things ready. And if you don't, Sally will."

"Gladly. We'll plan everything out. I don't know if Brent will break free from whatever he's doing, but I'd love for us to all be together."

He started to say goodbye, then paused. "Hey, did Sally tell you that a bunch of the local ladies are putting together a Christmas Eve potluck dinner?"

"You mean for the town? Tyler, that sounds wonderful. That's the best kind of celebration, when folks join together. Like they used to do up in Vermont." She'd been raised in a small New England town and his mother understood old-fashioned Yankee hospitality.

"We're in for brisket and whatever else you want to make. Or have Sally make," he added, laughing.

"Pies," she declared. "I haven't made my own pie for the holidays in over a decade, and it's time to refresh my skills. Put me down for two caramel-apple pies. I love the thought of an old-fashioned Christmas."

"It'll be great, Mom." Family here for the holidays. That hadn't happened in all the years he'd been living on the ranch. Maybe because his family hadn't wanted to rub the whole holiday thing in his face.

Now it seemed right. Normal. When was the last time he'd felt normal?

He hung up and went downstairs to find Sally. "So Hurricane Mary Clare is blowing into town on the twenty-third, I hear."

Sally laughed but didn't disagree. "It'll be great fun, having your parents here. And no small amount of pressure," she added honestly. "She asked me to have Dad come spend the holiday with us. Tyler, you come from good people."

He couldn't deny it, and they'd given him plenty of space to heal since losing Lisbeth. Maybe too much, because he'd been wallowing in self-pity for a long time. "The best. What can I help with?"

"Right now the best thing you can do is to get things straightened out about that house for Jessica and her little girl. I've got this here. George and Billy can handle the feed duties now that the cows are more accessible, but if I need lifting and carrying, I'll grab one of them. I don't want that young mother worrying one more minute than she has to. Being a widow is hard enough," she went on. She looked at Ty and sighed. "You didn't realize, did you?"

"She never said anything and I didn't want to ask or assume."

"She didn't say much to us, either, just that he'd passed on over a year ago."

He understood that harsh reality better than most. "I'll take care of things right now."

"And see if they want to come to supper tonight," she added. "I'm putting together chicken and biscuits, and nothing says welcome to a community like a pot of chicken and biscuits."

"I'll ask her." He grabbed his wallet and the online paperwork he'd printed earlier. He pulled away from the ranch, wishing there was a store nearby. He'd have bought flowers. Or chocolates. Or something nice and small just to show Jessica and Dovie that someone cared about them.

He pulled into her driveway a few minutes later.

Jessica was perched on the top of a ladder,

stringing lights along the upper gutter. Dovie was on the front porch, watching her mother with a wide smile. Jessica gave a little wave when he pulled in and exited the pickup truck.

The ladder tipped with the movement. Just slightly, but enough to have him grip the base tightly. "What if this fell with you on it? How would you get help?" he asked, and if he sounded like he was scolding… Well, there was good reason for it.

"Dovie, if we have an accident, what do you do?"

Dovie was watching from the porch and she waved her mother's phone, clutched in her little hand. "Call 911!"

"Perfect." He frowned up at Jessica. "So the kid becomes a witness to her mother's demise."

"We have adopted a no-worry policy here," Jessica told him as she fastened the last few inches of lights to the roof's edge. "God's in control and we'll do our best to be careful."

She made it sound easy.

You used to think it was easy. You believed, heart and soul, then one tragic accident knocked you off-kilter. Was that God's fault? Or human error magnified because you were behind the wheel?

He knew the answer to that. Admitting it was something altogether different.

"Done." She looked down. "Can you hand me that orange extension cord, please? Then this section of lights is all set."

He handed the cord up to her. She fastened the lights into the cord, then climbed down. "First section complete. Now we are on to porch garland."

"I'm so 'cited, Mommy!"

"Me, too," she told Dovie while Ty tipped the ladder down. "And you can help with the garland because you're just the right size."

Dovie clapped her mitten-clad hands together and beamed. "I will be the best helper ever!"

Jessica turned back to him once the ladder was down. He nudged the ladder with his foot. "Where'd you get this?" he asked.

"That back shed," she told him. "I didn't think there'd be anything in there, but I discovered a few handy things. A push lawn mower, some garden tools, this ladder and four outdoor extension cords. I hope you don't mind that I helped myself," she told him. "Is this stuff yours?"

"It's not. By the way, I brought you the paperwork to transfer the house back to you." He held up a folder he'd set on the hood of his pickup truck. "We'll get this sent in for filing today."

"Ty." She took his hands in hers and held his gaze. "Are you sure about this? Because it's a nice gesture and all, but probably too nice The least I can do is pay you what you paid for the house. The back taxes and whatever fees they added. Don't you think?"

He didn't think that at all. Gazing down, he was pretty sure that there was nothing too nice for this kindhearted woman. "No, ma'am." He purposely switched to a slow, lazy drawl. When she smiled, he knew his ploy had worked. "I think everything should start with nice. Don't you?"

She squeezed his hands in a sweet, silent message. "I do."

"Well, then, let's get this porch decorated and stuff done because I have another surprise in this folder." He opened it and held up a printed paper. "Tree permits. Are you ladies willing to take a ride in the truck and cut down some Christmas trees today?"

"Oh, yes!" Dovie scrambled half up the railing, excited. "I would love that so much, Mr. Ty! Mommy, can we? Please?"

"Well, since he asked in front of you and got your hopes up…" she scolded with a teasing tone, but she didn't look really annoyed.

"I may be guilty of employing every possible tactic to break down your defenses," he admitted.

"Let's get the outside decorated first. The radio said today's weather is a temporary respite, so Dovie and I decided to get this stuff done. Then we can enjoy it for the next few weeks."

"I'll put the ladder away for you." Ty lifted it. "Be right back."

"Oh, Mommy, can you believe it? We're going to the big woods to get a Christmas tree! With Mr. Ty!"

Her words didn't just catch his heart.

They captured it.

If nothing else came of this attraction, the thought that he'd been a help to a widow and her child took him back to no small number of sermons he'd preached years before. Sermons of love and forgiveness, of caring for the sick. The lame. The downtrodden. He'd been a good pastor. A good man.

But he'd fallen apart at his first major loss and had been unable to put himself back together.

Anger does that. It's not lack of faith that turns so many away. It's bold, robust anger when things spin out of our control, because humans like control.

He knew that. He'd always known that, so why, when it was his turn to suffer, had he turned away?

He came back to the front of the house, unsure of the answers but ready to face them. Find them. It was time.

"Can you hold this end of the garland, Ty?"

Jessica handed him one end. "And put a nail in the post right about there…" She marked the post with a little measuring tape and pencil. "I'll put marks on the other posts and we'll just hook the garland to the nails."

"Easy enough for a country boy like me," he told her, grinning. Once he'd driven the nails into place, he picked Dovie up and let her hook garland onto the nail. He let her repeat the procedure, one post at a time. When they were done, he stepped back so Dovie could see her handiwork.

"I can't even wait for it to get dark," she told him. Excitement for twinkle lights and all things Christmas brightened her big brown eyes.

And then she planted those mittened hands on either side of his face and kissed him. "Thank you, Mr. Ty! Thank you so much."

"Dovie…" Jessica started to caution her, but Ty shook his head.

"It's fine. She's managed to do what hundreds of cows haven't been able to do the last few years," he went on as he hugged the little girl. "She started making me feel downright good again. Got me thinking again, and that's a step in the right direction," he added, smiling. "I'm not sure how or why this whole mix-up happened, Jessica." He jutted his chin toward the house. "But I'm glad it did."

"Ty."

The single word held warning. She looked like she was going to caution him again, so he figured the best way to stop that was to take care of business. "This is done, right?"

She nodded.

"Let's go in and take care of the paperwork. That way I can drop it by the lawyer's office on my way back to the ranch this afternoon. He'll file the change of ownership with the town. And we can go get us a Christmas tree. Two, actually," he went on. "I got three permits, but Sally and her dad are having Christmas at the ranch, so I really only need two."

"Unless we cut one and donate it," she suggested. "I bet we could use it at the church. Oh, that would be a splendid idea," she told him, and the minute she said it, he realized she was right. He had the extra permit. Why not help the town?

They got the paperwork done while Dovie took care of gathering her layers of clothing in her very particular manner.

"This is a process," Jessica whispered to him as she brought two mugs of coffee to the table. "And it has to be just right."

"She didn't get this from you, I take it?" She set down the coffees and sat next to him. Close enough that the scent of floral soap, clean air and coffee made him wish she was closer.

"This is my mother, through and through," she told him. Regret deepened her voice. "She was a wonderful woman that Dovie never had the chance to know. I'm sorry about that, because my mom was amazing. Strong. Stalwart. Faithful. She never let things pull her off the right path, and it took me too long to follow in her footsteps."

"Don't you think that's normal, though?" he asked her.

She drew her brows in.

"Maybe when your mom was your age, she wobbled a bit, too. I think most of us do before we get older. Smarter. More solid. More experienced."

"Well, now, you sound too smart for words."

He laughed softly at her expression, then winced. "I'm the biggest work in progress there is. Some of us are too hardheaded to grab hold of that experiential learning stuff right off the bat."

"Life has a way, doesn't it?" She sipped her coffee as she watched Dovie match socks to her leggings and the snow pants. It took three pairs to find the right shades of pink and green to satisfy the little girl. "I should have paid attention to my mother more," she told him. Her voice was resigned. "She saw things I didn't want to see because I was on a mission to change the world. I married Dovie's father and moved west with him, but I was so naive." She frowned. "I'd been raised by a Caucasian mother and an Onondagan father. He was a great man who shared the history of our people with me, the Five Nations. How they found peace together. How they respected women. When I met Ben and he was so on fire to help his tribe, I joined in. Then I found myself in the middle of so much anger. I didn't understand what Ben was telling me before we married, how motivated he was to making things better. Or maybe I didn't understand how bad things were because I'd never experienced any of it."

"He sounds like he had a strong commitment."

She raised her eyes to his and he read the pain there. "He did. But not to me. Or to Dovie. And I discovered that too late. He was totally committed to the cause as he saw it. I think I was some kind of trophy to him, a middle-class Native American blend that he was teaching to be truly one of the people but there was only one way. His way. He wanted to see me immerse myself in the injustices of life. But that wasn't who I was, and that made things terrible."

"Jessica." He covered her hand with his. "I'm sorry. Real sorry."

"There were good people there," she told him. "Lots of them. And a lot of folks fighting a losing battle against substance abuse. His family refused to understand why I didn't want Dovie surrounded by all of that. They saw me as a spoiled outsider. When Ben's illness got real bad, they blocked me from seeing him. In the end, that was all right, because he wasn't the man I'd married. Sickness and anger had pushed him to be something else. Someone else."

Her story broke his heart, but the strength in her voice beckoned him. He couldn't imagine taking a woman like this for granted. But he'd met men from varying walks of life who'd behaved in a similar fashion. Many of them sat right up front in church, swollen with pride and self-importance.

"Perfect!" Dovie had pulled on the chosen socks and stood. She did a quick twirl that made them both smile.

"She's marvelous, isn't she?" Jessica asked softly as Dovie hummed a Christmas carol while drawing her snow pants on. "When Ben died, his family started lawsuits against the medical teams for insufficient care, and then against me, to claim custody of Dovie because she was their blood."

Ty couldn't believe that he'd heard her correctly. "They tried to get custody of her? From her own mother?" He whispered the words so Dovie wouldn't hear.

"Yes. I had to stay close by for a while to

go through all the court hearings. The minute I could leave, I did, making Ben's family very angry. Ben had been their bright hope for change. An educated, strong, articulate man. But the anger consumed him after we moved west. Getting sick was like the final straw. He moved in with his mother and uncle then, and that was all right, because I wasn't sure Dovie would be safe around him. I couldn't trust his reactions, which made them hate me even more."

Tyler couldn't imagine anyone hating her. Yet, he'd seen his share of family anger and civil unrest years before. That part he understood from his pastoral vocation.

"I think I'm ready!" Dovie had climbed into everything except her heavy jacket. "Can we bring hot chocolate with us?"

Jessica started to nod, but Ty interrupted. "How about if we get the trees, then come back here for hot chocolate?" he suggested. "I can get the tree set in a stand for you and make sure it's secure. Sound good?"

"Yes!"

The grown-ups hurried into their outdoor layers, and when they pulled into the forest a few minutes later, Dovie's eyes went wide. "I think these are the biggest trees ever, mister!"

"They are pretty big." He set her down and

withdrew his small chainsaw from the bed of the truck.

"Not a handsaw?" Jessica asked, and he tipped a pretend frown her way. "That's how they do it in the movies," she teased.

"That's like telling you to do your job with colored pencils," he told her. "This way, we get the job done and you have more time to decorate."

She laughed.

He liked the sound of it. He was pretty sure laughter had been in short supply the last few years, so making her laugh felt good.

And he couldn't deny that he enjoyed feeling good again.

Chapter Ten

꩜

Ty helped them wrestle the tree into the house after he lopped off another twelve inches from the trunk. He cut the extra branches from the bottom and was about to toss them into the truck bed for mulch when Jessica stopped him. "I think I'd like to use them for the nativity set."

"Oh. Great idea." He wasn't sure what she meant, but he piled the branches onto the porch. "Let's get this inside, okay?" He brought the Douglas fir in, and after they'd wrestled it into the living room, he examined the tree. "They seem to grow once we get them inside. Know what I mean?"

"It looks so big!" Dovie clapped her hands in glee while Jessica centered Sally's stand in the front window.

"Back it up," he advised her. "When the

branches relax, you're going to need that extra space by the window."

She slid it back, then helped Ty lift it into the holder. "It's amazing. I can't wait to decorate it," said Jessica. She reached out and gave him a hug. A hug he didn't want to end. "Thank you, Ty Carrington." She leaned back, but when he didn't release her completely, she smiled softly. "You've gone the distance to make us feel welcome here. I don't know how to thank you properly."

He grinned. "No thanks needed, ma'am. Seeing Dovie and you happy is plenty. And maybe some homemade brownies or cookies out at the ranch. The men and I get lonesome for homemade stuff like that. Sally's time is split these days. Of course we could make some ourselves, but Sally would not take kindly to what four men can do to a kitchen."

"Dovie and I love making cookies, so that's perfect," she told him. "Can we come by on Thursday?"

"Sounds fine to me, but Sally was hoping you ladies would be available for supper tonight. She made a pot of chicken and gravy, with her special biscuits, too."

"You had me at chicken and gravy," Jessica told him. She followed him to the door. "Thank you, Ty. We're very grateful."

"It's a pleasure, Jess." She smiled when he shortened her name, as if she liked the familiarity. "I'll see you gals around five thirty, all right?"

"We'll be there."

"And I've got an extra tree base at the ranch, one that should fit the bigger tree for the church."

"I'll bring it back with me tonight," she told him.

"Sounds good. See you later, Dovie."

She flew across the room and leaped into his arms. "Bye, Mr. Ty! I'll see you for supper, okay? With my mom," she added, as if she could get there any other way.

He left, laughing.

They waved from the window, and Jessica was reaching to unpack the strings of lights when a text came through from Ben's sister. Judge's ruling should come down any day. EJC Pharmaceuticals will not be having a happy holiday season this year. Thought you should know.

Why should she know or even care? She texted back quickly. I am not part of that lawsuit. I don't believe in making money off the deaths of others.

LuEllen's reply came back just as quick. You're part of it whether you like it or not. You were his wife. You had his daughter. You might want to remove yourself from us, but this is part of you. Part of your past. Own it.

Jessica stared at the reply.

She'd refused to take any part in suing the medical professionals involved in Ben's care. They'd tried so many things, but his cancer was a rare form of leukemia that hadn't responded to the usual treatments. That wasn't medicine's fault. That was life. And, sure, she hoped they'd continue to make advances in treatments, but how could she shake a fist and blame others for this?

She texted back swiftly. Leave Dovie and me out of this. We need nothing. We're doing fine. And I hope that the peace and joy of Christmas blesses all of you.

A nasty emoji was the only reply.

She erased the emoji so Dovie wouldn't accidentally see it, and put the phone away.

Ben's family wanted money. They wanted restitution. They wanted Ben's death to be someone's fault, but sometimes things just happened. She believed that.

Maybe she was naive, but there was nothing in that angry lawsuit for her or for her precious child.

They got the lights strung, then hung their two small boxes of ornaments, cute handmade things she'd done with her preschool daughter the previous year. And when she let Dovie hang the gifted ornaments from Sally and her father, the tree glistened. Their first Christmas tree in Idaho was absolutely beautiful.

"Oh, Mommy." Dovie breathed the words against Jessica's cheek as she held the little girl up when the tree was complete. The sun had started to set, and the glow of the twinkle lights brightened the porch and the room. "Isn't it the most beautiful tree ever?"

"It is, darling." She hugged Dovie, then set her down. "Grab your jacket and let's head out to Mr. Ty's house for supper."

"Can he come here to see our tree?" asked Dovie as she tugged her jacket on. "I think he'll like it a lot."

"How about we take him a picture of us in front of the tree, Lovie-Dovie?" She put the phone on selfie mode. "Our first Christmas selfie in Shepherd's Crossing." She reached out and snapped a picture of her and Dovie and the tree, then paused.

It was beautiful. The simple tree, the modest home, the humble surrounding…and her, with Dovie.

"I think he will really like that picture," said Dovie.

"I think he will, too." She sent him the photo,

and when they arrived at the ranch a few minutes later, the picture was the first thing he mentioned.

"Hey, gals." He opened the door wide for them to come in. His big old red dog moseyed their way, wagged his tail, then flopped on the rug near the fire, a perfect setting. "I love the Christmas picture you sent me."

"It was so beautiful!" Dovie grinned up at him, then went around the corner of the living room to pet the dog. "And I think Red's one of the very most nicest dogs I ever met, Mr. Ty."

"He's a good old boy." He smiled at her, petting the dog, then turned back to Jessica. "The tree came out great."

"It really did," she replied. She nodded toward the living room. "She's so excited, Ty. I know you said no thanks needed, but…" She reached up and kissed his cheek in gratitude.

He'd shaved recently. No rough stubble hit her lips. And when he turned slightly, then found her mouth with his, she lost herself in his arms. His kiss. The scent of him, piney and rugged with hints of wood smoke.

She drew back too soon. "I told myself we wouldn't do this," she scolded. "I don't want or need a broken heart, and I have to stay strong and focused for her."

"I find that kissing helps me do that," he replied.

She batted his arm lightly and he laughed. Then he hugged her. He hugged her so perfectly that she knew she could live her life in this man's arms forever and not regret a single moment.

Of course that was preposterous because they had just met. Yet, it felt absolutely right.

"I like this, Jess." He whispered the words against her cheek. Her ear.

"But—"

"Let's table the concerns for the moment." He leaned back and smiled down at her, then released her. "Let's eat, and we'll worry about the rest later. Nothing seems as worrisome after chicken and biscuits."

He was right.

Sally and the other men joined them for supper, a monster-sized pot of gravy and pulled chicken. And when Sally brought out a coconut cake for dessert, it was all Jessica could do to keep herself from applauding. "Two of my favorite things in this world, Sally. Chicken and biscuits and coconut cake. Or pie. Coconut anything."

"That makes you fine people in my book, because simple good food is never a bad thing," she declared, smiling. "Now, does Miss Dovie like coconut, too?"

Dovie shook her head, but didn't frown. "No, thank you."

"Well, darlin', how about a dish of ice cream for you?"

"I love ice cream!" Dovie perked up instantly. "But not with bumps."

"Bumps?" The table full of people looked to Jessica for explanation.

"Nuts. Chunks of chocolate. Chunks of anything. My little White Dove is a connoisseur of smooth and silky ice cream."

"No bumps." Ty laughed as he moved to get the ice cream. "How about vanilla, kid?"

"I love it so much!"

"There you go." He scooped out a serving, then realized he was feeding a four-year-old and put half of it back. "No bumps."

"Thank you, mister!"

The men laughed. Once they finished their cake, they said their goodbyes to her and Dovie, and thumped Ty on the back.

"A nice group of men," she noted when the table had emptied.

"They know their cows. And the ranch. And the seasons."

"'To every thing there is a season, and a time for every purpose under the heaven.'"

"Ecclesiastes 3," he said. "A lesson in truth for all ages." He was moving dishes to the counter, and when Sally tried to shoo him away, he balked. "You go sit. You've been running around all day. I've got this."

"*We've* got this," corrected Jessica. "It's got to be almost fun to clean up a big, gorgeous kitchen like this."

"Almost." Sally lifted a skeptical brow her way, and she laughed.

"I hear you. You cooked. We clean. Makes sense to me."

"I won't argue because these dogs are barkin' loud tonight." She indicated her feet. "Thank you, both. And, Ty, if you have time this next week to go see a few places in town with me, I'd appreciate it. I haven't ever bought a house on my own, and Dad's not up to shopping around."

"I'll be glad to."

Sally went to her room. Dovie finished her ice cream and curled up in front of a Christmas cartoon TV special with Red, and Jessica and Ty cleaned up the kitchen in short minutes. Just like that, the night was over. Only she didn't want it to be over. And she didn't want to ponder the reasons why.

Chapter Eleven

Ty saw Jessica glance at her watch once they finished straightening the kitchen. That meant he was running out of time, but Dovie saved the day.

"Mr. Ty! I think your tree looks so dark and lonely out here, don't you? Like it's waiting for someone to love it?"

"Dovie—"

Ty interrupted Jessica's caution because Dovie was right. "It does look pretty somber, doesn't it?"

"We can make it beautiful, just like ours!" She gripped his hand, leading him forward. "I'm like the very best helper. My mom said so!"

"Ty."

Jessica's caution drew his attention.

"We shouldn't intrude on family things like this." She motioned toward the tree. "Dovie doesn't understand that sometimes families have traditions about these things."

"I suggest a compromise," he offered. If she agreed, they wouldn't leave quite so soon. "I'd love help with the lights. They can be a pain. Then we can leave the ornaments for my mother. She loves that stuff. And there's not a whole lot of time between when they arrive and Christmas. If we got the lights done, that would be a huge help to me."

She tapped her watch. "Thirty minutes, Dovie. I've got work to finish tonight, okay?"

"Thank you, Mommy!" She skipped over to the tree, ready to get started.

He didn't like that Jessica had to stay up late to complete her work. And yet he liked that she took pride in everything she did. With the humble house. With her job. With Dovie.

They finished the tree lights, but before they went home he brought Dovie a brightly wrapped package. "Miss Dovie?" He held out the box. "A pre-Christmas present."

"For me?" Eyes wide, she dashed his way. "But it's not Christmas yet."

"This is one of those presents that's best given before Christmas," he told her.

She sought her mother's permission. When Jessica nodded, Dovie took a seat on the floor and carefully unwrapped the package.

"Oh, Mr. Ty." She sighed, then gave a little shriek of delight when she saw the green ceramic tree. "It is so beautiful. I love it so much, and I will take such good care of it!" She set the box aside and hugged him.

The hug unleashed his heart and maybe shook loose his soul. Too soon it was time to let them both go.

He helped Dovie into her boots while Jessica dressed for the cold night. "I can drive you guys home." It was a silly offer, but he made it anyway.

"And leave my car here?" she teased him, smiling.

It felt wrong to let them go into the winter's night on their own.

"We're fine, Ty. Not our first rodeo. We've got this."

"I know." He'd finished Dovie's boots. She stomped them onto the floor to make sure her little feet were snugged down. "That doesn't make it feel right, Jess."

He gazed up at her, then stood.

Now she looked up at him.

He wanted to kiss her again. He wanted to hold her, to talk about the sadness he glimpsed in her eyes sometimes. He wanted to tell her about Lisbeth and the baby, about how mad he'd been at God for so long, because he was pretty sure she'd understand.

"We're absolutely fine," she assured him. "Gotta go. Thank you, Ty. It was a wonderful night." She took Dovie's hand.

"We'll see you soon, okay?" Dovie grinned up at him, winning more of his heart. "Bye, Red!" She leaned around the corner and called to the floppy-eared dog, "Love you!"

The innocent love of a child. The sweet faith, unspoiled.

He bent and kissed her cheek. "Bye, Miss Lovie-Dovie."

She laughed and kissed him right back. "Bye, mister!"

"See you Thursday," Jessica reminded him.

He wanted to hug her again. Kiss her, too. But Dovie was there. "See you then."

He watched as their car pulled away, then studied the light-studded tree in the broad window of the great room.

It looked like Christmas, and the fresh piney scent made it smell like Christmas, too.

He hadn't put up a tree since the accident. Since walking away from his church, his congregation. He hadn't cared about God for years.

Now he did. He cared because he saw the light of faith in Jessica's eyes, in her words, in her smile. Tragedy had struck her and she hadn't run. She hadn't cast blame. She'd stayed stoic and strong. Because she had Dovie?

He didn't know.

He only knew he needed to be more like that. Depend on God. On faith. On grace.

He smiled at the thought as his father's ringtone signaled a call. "Hey, Dad. What's up?"

"I wanted you to know that I've got a bunch of Christmas packages coming there. Can you and Sally tuck them out of sight until we arrive?" His father sounded off, somehow. Tired.

"I'm on it. Everything okay? What's going on?"

His father sighed.

E.J. Carrington never sighed. He studied. He worked. He engineered. He hired and fired the best of the best in every biomedical field to keep the company's cutting edge against disease.

"That big lawsuit claiming discrimination that got filed nearly two years back? The judge is scheduled to give his verdict before Christmas."

A family had sued the company not because the drug had adverse effects, but because their patient didn't make it into a clinical trial for a newly developed immunotherapeutic drug for resistant leukemias. They'd accused the company of discrimination. "Rough timing on a lot of fronts."

"It is," E.J. agreed. "I wish those folks knew

how my heart breaks every time a treatment gets close but not close enough. How I'd have given anything to have the right circumstances to save their family member. It just wasn't right according to the doctors, and they can only qualify people under the strictest conditions."

"I know, Dad."

"And seven plaintiffs," he went on. "What kind of case has seven plaintiffs? The Lambert one, that's what. Mother, uncle, sisters, wife, child. It's as if everybody wants a piece of the pie."

"I expect they're all hurting."

"That part I understand," E.J. agreed. "The wife and child, Jessica and Mary White Dove, those two I get. The mother, too. But where do the rest come in?"

Tyler couldn't focus on the question because he was too intent on the statement before.

Jessica. Mary White Dove. Lambert.

It couldn't be, and yet… Her husband had died. She'd showed up here, claiming ownership of one of their properties, and just happened to be a primary plaintiff in a lawsuit against his family's company, EJC Pharmaceuticals.

His heart started to pound.

Had she come here intentionally? To gain sympathy? What other answer could there be? It couldn't be coincidence that had brought her and Dovie to Shepherd's Crossing. It had to be a plan, right? How else could so many things seamlessly fall into place? And he'd fallen for her sweet facade, her charm, her supposed integrity. He'd fallen for it completely.

Was the whole thing a ruse?

It couldn't be. Not with her. Not with Jessica.

Yet, what else could it be?

He said goodbye to his father, went to the side porch and stepped out. He needed air. He needed cold, clean, fresh air, the kind that would wake him up out of this stupid, foolish, bad dream, because there was no way his father could have just named Jessica and Dovie in a major lawsuit worth millions.

But he had.

Ty stared at the stars.

He didn't feel the cold. He couldn't say if it was windy or calm, because it didn't matter. It didn't matter because everything that had started to matter again to him just came crashing down.

You gave her a house.

Oh, man.

What would his family say when they realized what he'd done? Not that the house had been a huge outlay of cash. It wasn't. Or that they couldn't buy other town properties. He and Eric had already gone over that.

But he'd fallen for her lies, signed the house over to her, set her up for Christmas…

Fallen for her.

Completely. Utterly. In the space of a couple of weeks.

Crazy, yes. He knew that. Knew it more now that he realized he'd been played and hung out to dry.

His father had said the judge's ruling was due soon.

She'd quoted the Bible to him. She'd made him think. Laugh. Help. Yearn.

And maybe that was the worst of all, because he'd been numb for years. She had ended that. Now her duplicity began it all again. His fault, though. She hadn't just played him. He'd let himself be played.

He went to bed determined to stay away. He'd avoided being part of the community for several years. It wasn't even really a hardship to do it again.

Chapter Twelve

Ranch work keeping me tied up the rest of this week. Sorry about Thursday.

Jessica read the message three times.

No real emotion. No explanation. Nothing that indicated those growing feelings, those shared kisses.

There you go, trying to read more into things than you should. Men sneak kisses all the time, don't they? Now you know better.

Her brain was right to scold her. She'd known better last night, yet there she was, kissing Tyler Carrington and loving it. Maybe loving him. Starting to, anyway, so this was as much her fault because she knew better.

She and Dovie set up the manger. She had some florist foam in a box from Sally. She cut it to fit a long rectangular baking dish, then set it behind the manger. She and Dovie tucked thin branches of the trimmed evergreen tree, holly from the backyard bush, plain, thin sticks and tiny red ribbons in.

"That's so beautiful, Mommy." Dovie leaned her head against Jessica's cheek Wednesday night. "It's like a perfect place for baby Jesus to get borned."

It wasn't perfect.

Jess knew that.

What young mother would choose a cave for her newborn son? Or animal roommates? No clothing or diapers for the little fellow.

Yet Mary had pushed through the hardship. Jesus had thrived. She, Joseph and Jesus had made their way through life with purpose, and that was the example Jessica was determined to follow.

She kept Dovie busy the next few days, but called Lizzie on Friday to explain about the tree.

"It's here, at the church, and I've got a stand for it, but I can't set it up myself," she told her.

"Ty bought the church a tree?" Lizzie sounded surprised.

"Yes. And he had an extra stand he's letting us borrow."

"But he's not available to help put it in place." Lizzie's voice took on a thoughtful tone, the kind that meant she was reading between the lines.

"Busy, I'm sure. A big ranch is a lot of work." Jessica made the excuse easily. Not for him. For her and Dovie, because the last thing she needed was sympathy over her foolishness. She hadn't come to Shepherd's Crossing to find romance. She'd come to find peace from the constant in-fighting of Ben's family.

"Mel and I have time right now and we'll grab Char on the way," said Lizzie. Their younger sister was a local big animal veterinarian. "We'll get this done so we can have it lit this Sunday. We'll meet you in ten minutes. Okay?"

"Yes."

Four women arrived ten minutes later. Corrie Satterly waved her hands at Lizzie. "You watch Zeke and Dovie. I am not havin' one of my girls haulin' trees around when she's with child. We've got this."

In fifteen minutes they had the tree screwed into the holder, ready for lights. An hour later the lights were strung, ready to be a backdrop for their Advent and Christmas services.

"We did it." Melonie high-fived Jessica and Charlotte. "I'm so glad you thought of it."

"Well, Mr. Ty was the one who thinked it."

Jessica's heart scrunched as Dovie outed them completely.

"Only he doesn't come to see us anymore and

I really miss him because he's our friend. And I like having supper with him and Red."

"Red?" Lizzie asked, and when Lizzie directed her attention to Jessica, she had to answer.

"Ty's dog. A big, reddish golden retriever."

"Ah. But you haven't seen Ty or the dog in a few days?"

About now the thought of muzzling one smart child appealed to Jessica, but she was pretty sure that was illegal. "No biggie. We've been on our own for a while," she told the women.

"Except that I've been here seven months and I've never seen Ty happier than he's been the past two weeks. Talking with people. Laughing. Joining in." Lizzie drew her brow down. "So what changed?"

Jessica put up her hands in surrender as they headed to the church door. "Who knows? I've come to the conclusion that men are a mystery, and my time is better used focusing on raising a wonderful daughter. Forget the romance."

Melonie frowned over her shoulder as she bent to lock the church door. "Sounds like she's got it bad."

"Real bad," added Charlotte.

"So how can we help?" Lizzie wondered out loud as Zeke and Dovie twirled in the freshly falling snow.

"No need for anything. I'm fine, really," she

assured all four of them. "But it's actually a blessing to be able to talk to women about this. I've missed having girlfriends around. So, thank you. And now I'm going to get Dovie home for a quick bath and supper, because there's a Christmas special on tonight and we're going to have movie time."

Lizzie smiled. "It sounds marvelous." Then she stepped closer to Jessica and took one hand. "I'm going to make a suggestion," she explained in a soft voice. "It's up to you what to do with it, but I think you should talk to him. Find out what's up."

"Too embarrassing," Jessica declared quickly.

"Maybe," acknowledged Lizzie. "But he wasn't just toying with one heart." She nodded in Dovie's direction. "And that's worth a scolding or two."

She thought about Lizzie's words that night, and the next day, too. When Lizzie called to see if she could take Dovie to a movie with Zeke, Jessica quickly said yes.

Five minutes after she dropped Dovie at Pine Ridge Ranch, she pulled into Carrington Acres.

She hurried out of the car before she lost her nerve, then climbed the steps and crossed to the front door. She knocked.

No one answered.

She rang the bell.

Red began barking. He came to the door, tail wagging, spotted her through the window and barked some more.

Ty's truck was here. Was he deliberately not answering the door?

Or was he out working?

She moved around the house to the first barn and spotted George. "Is Ty out here?" she asked.

"Toward the back of the horse barn, miss."

She thanked him and went that way. There he was, in the back, rebuilding a stall gate. Whistling as if he hadn't a care in the world.

"Ty."

He turned quickly. First he looked surprised, then unhappy. "I wasn't expecting you."

"I know." She moved forward. She hadn't come to fight. She deplored fighting and drama. But she had come to say her piece. She folded her arms both as a defense and to ward off the cold wind sweeping through the far end of the barn. "I don't know what's going on with you," she began. "And that's fine. I don't need to know. But I have a little girl who doesn't understand why her friend Mr. Ty was a big part of her life and then suddenly dropped off the radar. I get it, Ty." She locked her eyes on his. "I'm a grown woman. But four-year-old hearts are much more easily broken and confused, so the next time you—"

He stared at her as if dumbfounded that she didn't get it. "You're suing my father."

Jessica stopped talking.

"You're suing my father over the death of your husband. And you've even brought that sweet little girl's name into it."

"I don't—" She started to speak, but didn't have a real clue what to say.

"Don't sugarcoat it, Jessica, don't make excuses." He wiped his hands on a well-worn barn towel. "I'm already feeling stupid for falling for the whole thing. The house, the proximity, quoting scripture, which means you probably know that I was a pastor at one time."

She raised a hand to stop him. "I have no idea what you're talking about. I'm suing no one. Over anything. And if you're talking about the lawsuit Ben's mother and family instigated over his treatment, that's got nothing to do with me. But what does your father have to do with any of this?"

"EJC Pharmaceuticals." When she didn't respond, he went on, "E.J. Carrington is my father. He owns the company."

"Your father." She stared at him, started to talk, then paused. "Wait. You think I set this up?"

"You come to town. Set up housekeeping in a house we bought. Pretend to know nothing about us. And yet your name is on the lawsuit. And Dovie's name, too."

"And you believed all this." She took a deep breath to fight back angry tears. "You decided I'd come north to weasel my way into the EJC fortune."

He stayed silent, but his face said enough.

"You didn't have the decency to ask about it. You assumed. Well, here's the real story, Ty." She had to squeeze her hands into tight fists to not lash out at him. "I married a man who loved his cause far more than he loved me. I discovered that too late, and when things didn't go his way, he got violent. And then he got terminally ill, so I stayed to help nurse him through the worst of it. When he died, his family didn't just sue your father's company. They sued me, trying to take custody of my daughter. There I was, my mother had passed away, my marriage was a sham, Ben had died and I had to wrangle with the court system to keep my daughter because tribal law said she should stay with them. And with the problems their community faced every day, I couldn't stay there. It wasn't an option. When the courts denied their petition, I came here to take over my aunt's house. So before you go throwing around accusations, maybe you could have had the decency to do some homework. Or at least ask me. Because if you had, I'd have explained it all to you."

She turned on her heel and started to walk away.

"Jessica."

She didn't turn back. She couldn't.

Why would he assume such things when a fairly simple conversation would have cleared things up? When she got to the door, she turned, briefly. "And for the record, I've sent two written requests to have my name removed from that lawsuit. I didn't put my name on it, my former mother-in-law did. If it wasn't done, that's because Ben's family is hoping to get some sympathy for the grieving wife and child for a bigger payout. When all I want is to raise my child in a sweet, faith-filled community. That's my goal in life, Ty. And never in my wildest dreams did I think it would be this difficult." She walked back to her car, but not with her head down.

No. Never again.

Chin up, she crossed the graveled yard, then climbed into her car. And when she did, she put it into Reverse and drove away. Not once did she look back.

Half a story.

Funny how the guy who used to counsel people on getting all the facts before leaping to conclusions had just messed up his life by believing half a story.

He followed her to the edge of the barn. George cleared his throat and Ty looked his way. "I'd be letting that boiling pot go to simmer for a while," he told Ty. "Give her time to cool off."

"She shouldn't cool off. She should probably hate me the rest of her days. How did I mess up that badly?"

"Well, there's two things," the older man told him as he sanded rust from the barn door hinges. "You're sorely out of practice."

That was a fact.

"And you used to base everything you did in faith," George continued. "When you walked away from that, you lost something, Ty. And it's not like I didn't want to talk to you about it, but there was no right time till now. You were so mad."

George was right. Anger had pretty much consumed him.

"You've got to get over being mad sometime. Move on. Reach out. You finally start to do that, and along comes a hurdle and you caved."

Ty cringed at the truth in those words.

"It's time to stop caving. It's time to grab hold again, but you do that young woman no good if you don't make your peace with God. He didn't take your wife and baby. A wretched accident was to blame. I ain't sayin' it's fair, because it ain't, but it's life. And we have to live it. And now I'm takin' these old bones home for a good soak because that north wind is sharp today."

George left Ty alone. Sally was with her father. He walked into the house.

Red raced his way, tail wagging. He went to the door, excited, then back to Ty, as if telling him Jessica had come calling.

He needed to go see her.

But George was right. He needed to get his head on straight first, because he'd lost it when Lisbeth died. And then he'd let things lie fallow way too long.

He called the new pastor of his old church, and when he explained the situation, the pastor invited him to join them for the following weekend. He accepted the offer because before he dared embrace the present, he needed to make peace with the past. He'd get back home before his family's arrival. And maybe by then Jessica would be willing to hear him out, and if not...?

He'd keep trying, because he'd be a fool not to. He only wished he'd realized that a few days before.

Chapter Thirteen

The stage was set for a beautiful Christmas two weeks later. Volunteers had set up donated tables in the small firehouse down the road from the church. Borrowed tablecloths hid any imperfections, and votives in Mason jars lit each table. Sprigs of evergreen and holly formed rings around the jars, and Melonie had set red and gold ribbons into the greenery while Heath had strung three swaths of garland across the room. They'd wired pine cones and ribbon to the garlands, and when they were done, the whole room seemed ready for a party.

People began arriving just before two o'clock. They'd have three hours of feasting and cleanup before making the trek to the church.

"Do I get to hold my own candle? For real?" Dovie asked for the third time.

"As long as you're careful. And we'll sing hymns and make hearts happy."

"Because baby Jesus is having His birthday!" She reached up and clasped Jessica's hand, then let go and raced away. "Mr. Ty! Mr. Ty! I'm so glad to see you, mister! I've missed you so much."

There was no way that Jessica could stop her. She had a casserole in one arm and a bag of rolls in the other.

Dovie leaped into Ty's arms as if she belonged there, and when he snuggled her close and kissed her hair, Jessica wasn't immune to the beautiful setting. A tall, rugged cowboy, a pigtailed little girl, falling snow and Christmas.

But she'd found out that looks can be deceiving, so she kept her face expressionless as she moved forward. "Dovie. We don't jump on people."

"Well, maybe 'cept Mr. Ty," Dovie explained. "Because he's our friend."

Jessica wasn't about to explain otherwise. It was Christmas and folks were arriving, but when she turned to go inside, Ty put a hand on her shoulder. "Can we talk later, Jessica? Please?"

"It's Christmas, Ty. My priorities are right where they should be." She indicated her daughter with a glance. "With God and Dovie." She walked inside. He hadn't texted, messaged, called or stopped by to talk before now. No way was she giving this poignant Christmas Eve over to romance gone bad. Tonight was about faith, hope and love. Totally.

People were bustling around inside. A middle-aged woman with honey-brown hair and a take-charge demeanor was in deep discussion with Corrie about desserts. Jessica plugged her slow cooker full of sausage stuffing into an extended outlet and set the rolls on the table.

Ty had come in with Dovie, looking way too natural in his caretaker's role.

She turned her attention elsewhere intentionally, but then the brown-haired woman came her way. "Are you Jessica?" she asked.

A man joined them. Not as tall as Ty, but he looked enough like him to know that this must be his father, E.J. Carrington.

Her pulse ramped up.

This was the man Ben's family had sued. Not him personally, but his pharmaceutical company. And they hadn't been asking for small change, either. She took a deep breath, unsure what to say, then realized she didn't need to say a word.

"Miss Lambert."

She nodded.

He took her hand in both of his and gazed right into her eyes. "I'm E.J. Carrington, Miss

Lambert, and I wanted to take a moment to personally express my condolences for your loss."

"Mr. Carrington, I—" What could she say? The judge had found in the company's favor a few days before and Ben's family had been left with nothing but court costs and lawyer fees, none of which made them happy.

He seemed to understand her dilemma. "Words aren't necessary. It's a terrible thing to lose a loved one and emotions run high. Our grief—" he motioned to his wife "—is that we still don't have the perfect combination to stop cancer in its tracks. We will someday," he continued with the same kind of confident voice she'd seen in his son. "But it's not there yet, and your late husband wasn't a good candidate. Although I'm sure that wasn't what the family wanted to hear."

"Thank you, sir. I understood. The doctors were clear about the parameters required, but my husband and his family were quite upset. He made it clear that he wanted EJC Pharmaceuticals to pay for keeping him out of the program."

Ty's father grimaced. "It's hard to be so close and not there yet. To have things work on one person but not others just brings more questions."

"That will have eventual answers," his wife said. "Soon, my love."

He accepted her gracious assurance with a nod. "With God's help."

The chime of a soft bell drew their attention.

The small crowd turned toward the front. Lizzie Caufield held up a hand for quiet. "I promised my husband I wouldn't be up here making a speech while the food got cold, but we would like to say grace before we start filling our plates. Ty Carrington, will you do the honor? Please?"

Jessica was surprised to hear Lizzie call Ty's name, and even more surprised when he went forward, still carrying her daughter. "Dearest Lord," he began, head bowed. "We thank You for this food today, the work of human hands. We thank You for the warmth of this building, a place for us to gather as one. But mostly we thank You for the gift of Your son, our Lord and Savior, Jesus Christ. A tiny baby, born in a stable and laid in a manger. Dear Lord, from such humble beginnings came the most amazing greatness we've ever known, and we thank You for it on this beautiful celebration of Christmas. Amen."

The gathered crowd answered soundly, "Amen."

"Oh, that was such a very most lovely prayer, Mr. Ty!" Dovie clapped her two hands against Ty's cheeks as Jessica moved forward to get her. "I think it's time to eat now, and can you eat with my mom and me? Like we did a long time ago?" she asked. To a four-year-old, weeks were akin to eternity. "That would be so special, don't you think?"

"I expect Ty would like to eat with his mom and dad," Jessica suggested. "They came a long way to see him."

"I've got it!" Dovie tried to snap her fingers as if hit with a brilliant idea. "We can just sit with them, okay?" The common sense of the situation wasn't lost on her. "That way we can all be together."

"She makes a valid point." Ty gazed down at Jessica, as if she meant something. As if he wanted her to mean something.

She'd figured out the truth earlier in the month, but arguing at a Christmas celebration would be foolish.

"We'd be honored." She took a seat across from Ty's mother, and by the time the meal was over, she realized two things.

First, that she hadn't come close to getting over her attraction to Ty.

And second, that his mother was about the nicest person on the planet.

When the meal was complete, Jessica moved to the sink on the far wall. Each person was taking home their own dishes, but there was still a generous mound of things to be rinsed and washed here in the hall.

"You get away from there, young lady." Mary Clare Carrington didn't quite elbow Jessica out of the way, but it came close.

"Nonsense, you've got your two sons here with you and you're from out of town," Jessica insisted. "I've got this."

"Exactly why I'm stepping in with Eric." Mary Clare waved her oldest son over. "He's been in Colorado so there's no better way to catch up on things than over a sink of hot, soapy water."

"The sad part is she believes the stuff she spews." Eric feigned fear. "We do whatever's necessary to keep her happy."

Mary Clare pitched a towel at him and shooed Jessica away. "You go mingle," she told her. "Young mothers never get enough time to mingle these days. Mingling is good."

It wasn't just good.

It was wonderful. To be part of this gathering, to have helped plan and implement a town celebration. Sure, the turnout wasn't huge, but it was solid.

She was watching Dovie do a kids sing-along when Ty came up behind her.

She didn't need to look to know it was him.

She sensed it. The scent. The size. The hint of his breath touching her hair. Oh, she knew it all right, and absolutely, positively ignored it because no one would ever be allowed to make assumptions about her. Not now. Not ever.

"Jessica."

She kept her gaze trained firmly ahead. "Yes?"

"I'm sorry."

Oh, please. She didn't turn, didn't shift, didn't move a muscle. "For assuming I was a money-hungry woman trying to weasel her way into your heart? Or that I came here to insert myself and my daughter into the family's good graces for my own self-benefit? Or that I somehow knew you had commandeered my aunt's home for pennies on the dollar, when the county actually had no clue that I owned the property, or that I came here to gain sympathy for the loss of a man who turned out to be much less than I'd hoped and dreamed as a stargazing younger woman. Which one would it be, Ty?"

"Everything, Jessica."

The way he said it—like he was truly sorry—made her almost turn, but she wasn't about to let the sweet sentiment of the holiday mess with her head. "Then thank you. I appreciate it."

He moved in front of her, a little more insistent now. "We need to talk."

"I disagree."

"Come for Christmas dinner tomorrow."

And mess up the holy day with her daughter?

Not going to happen. "We're fine on our own. But thank you for the invitation. And now—" she slipped around him as Lizzie rang the soft chime once more "—I think it's time for the church walk."

She didn't look back at him. She didn't dare. A part of her longed to turn around. Say she forgave him. Smile up at him like she had those first short weeks.

But no one got to mess with her heart anymore. Ever. She helped get the younger kids ready for the candlelit trek up the road. When they were all dressed in outdoor clothes and lined up, it was Tyler who addressed the group from the front of the line. "In the old days," he told them, "we would have carried candles. Or oil lamps, like those women of the Bible. While today's light is different." He held up his Mason jar with a flickering battery-lit candle inside. "The tradition remains the same. That we'll walk together as a town to light up the church as the Light of Christ comes into the world."

And when he began leading the procession down the road to the scuffed-up church, his words came back to her. *You probably know that I was a pastor at one time...*

She hadn't then. But she saw it now.

Mary Clare fell into step on one side of Dovie. She smiled down at the little girl, then sighed.

"I didn't think I'd ever see my son lead a church again. When he lost his family, he lost his faith right along with it."

Lost his family? Jessica couldn't hide her surprise. "I didn't know that."

"Well, it was years ago, but the heart's an unreliable thing, isn't it? Strong in some ways, fragile in others. To see him conduct a service again, leading folks into church, I can honestly say this is one of the happiest days of my life. It's like that, isn't it?" She aimed a smile at a very animated Dovie as she sang "O Come, All Ye Faithful" with great gusto. "We want our children safe and happy, full of love for God. Anything else is window dressing," she told Jessica. "But those three things keep a mother's heart calm."

When they filed into the church, awash in flickering lights, someone turned on the tree they'd decorated two weeks before.

It shone like a star in the night, a reminder of God's love for His people. A child, born in poverty, for all the world to see.

Ty led the service. And when he first approached the podium, Dovie couldn't contain her excitement. "Look, Mommy!" She half shouted the words, plenty loud enough for everyone to hear, and the sound of soft laughter rose from the small gathering. "Right up there, Mommy, see him? It's our Mr. Ty!"

He smiled down at Dovie. And then…

From the pulpit, Tyler Carrington turned those big blue eyes on Jessica.

Her heart fluttered.

She scolded it roundly.

Her pulse sped up.

She ignored it.

And when her palms grew damp, she swiped them against the woven wool of her good coat.

She tried to focus on the homily.

She couldn't. She could only focus on him, the man, tall and kind and true, when he asked for her forgiveness. She'd brushed it off as if it was nothing. Hearing him tell the story of Christmas from a father's viewpoint, of his pain at losing his wife and his unborn child, she realized there was more to his story. And that only a foolish woman would shrug off someone like that.

She'd been foolish once. Was she repeating the mistake? Or moving on?

Folks gathered around him at the end of the beautiful service.

It made her heart happy to see it. To see joy in his face, in his eyes, in his stance.

She bade the Caufields and the Fitzgeralds a merry Christmas and walked Dovie home.

"It was so beautiful, wasn't it, Mommy?" Dovie danced ahead, trying to catch the few scattered snowflakes with her tongue. "So very, very nice!"

"It was." Jessica opened the door. Warmth hit them squarely, a welcome feeling, but as Dovie unfastened the buttons on her little dress-up coat, a familiar figure came their way.

She let Dovie go in while she waited for Ty on the porch.

The last cars were pulling away from the church. Lights still glowed from within, and the outdoor lights gleamed, too. For the first time since she'd moved here, the little church didn't look forlorn.

It looked cheerful and inviting. Kind of like the man coming her way. He climbed the scuffed steps and paused. "Jessica."

That voice. That gaze. Those eyes, holding hers. "It was a beautiful service, Ty."

He smiled. "It was. I wasn't sure if I could still do it. Get up and talk to people about God. About faith. About believing."

"But you did."

"I had to." He reached out and took her hands in his. "When I realized what I'd done, how I almost expected you to be too good to be true, I saw that it wasn't you who needed help. It was me. And so I went back to my old church post, the one I abandoned when I lost my family and I asked their forgiveness."

"I'm sure they understood." She squeezed his hands lightly. "Who wouldn't?"

"I needed the closure more than they did."

She'd gone through a similar emotion when she lost her mother because there were too many lost opportunities. Too many missed chances to say what needed to be said. "I know how that is."

"Well." He gripped her hands lightly, but with a firm touch. A masculine touch. "I knew you did. I'm here to ask you again, Jessica Lambert. To forgive me. And if you don't forgive me now, then I'll just keep right on showing up, out of the blue, asking again. And again. Because nothing would make this cowboy happier than putting those harsh words behind us. So we can make room for sweeter things, Jess."

He cupped her face with his hands. Then he gave her such a sweet and gentle smile that her heart practically jumped ship to become not her heart. But his heart. "I forgive you."

"Good." His lips touched hers in a beautiful kiss. A Christmas kiss. Then he pulled her close to him, wrapped in his embrace. "Come have dinner with us tomorrow. Please? I want my parents to get to know you. To get to know Dovie. To see how wonderful it all is."

"Mr. Ty! Mr. Ty, you came to see us and you did

such a really, really nice job in the church, and..."
Dovie stepped onto the porch, then planted her
two small hands on tiny hips. "I didn't even know
that you could do that stuff, not one little bit! How
very exciting was that, I ask you?"

He laughed and gathered her up in one strong
arm and kept the other snug around Jess's shoulders. "Very exciting. And very nice to have a
church service right here, together. Like it should
be, Lovie-Dovie."

She beamed at him, then her mother, then
hugged them both. "'Zactly what I was thinking, too. Merry Christmas, Mr. Ty!"

He kissed Dovie's cheek, then Jessica's. "The
merriest one ever."

"Agreed." Jessica made a face. "Has anyone
else noticed that it's cold out here?"

"I had noticed that." Ty grinned.

"Well, let's have our hot chocolate, okay?"
Dovie turned back toward Ty. "Mommy always
makes me hot chocolate with whipped cream
on Christmas Eve because it's the most special
night of all."

Ty set Dovie down. She skipped through the
door, laughing and singing. Then he turned back
to Jessica one last time before they went in. "She's
right, you know." He kissed her once more. "This
is the most special night of all. Agreed?"

He lifted one gorgeous eyebrow, a look she'd loved from day one. She smiled, leaned up and kissed him right back. "Agreed."

* * * * *

Dear Reader,

I love Christmas. My whole family loves Christmas. It's the season of light. A time of expectation. But we've got a big family, and we've known sorrow. A grieving heart might find the joyous lilt of holidays difficult. An angry heart has it even harder. Ty Carrington blamed himself for a tragic accident. He didn't see that his actions saved a child, because they cost him his family. Jessica Lambert sees things differently. She sees God's timing in everything, and while she has regrets, her buoyant, faithful nature pushes her forward.

It was an absolute pleasure to write this story and to work with Linda Goodnight, a dear and beautiful friend. Both Linda and I know that life comes complete with joy and pain, with love and sorrow. Anyone who risks love, risks loss. But God is good, and this beautiful story blesses the characters and the readers with the beauty of self-forgiveness and God's perfect timing at a much-treasured time of year.

Thank you for reading this sweet book! I love hearing from readers. Email me at loganherne@

gmail.com or stop by my website, www.ruthlo-ganherne.com. Friend me on Facebook, where I love to play and pray with readers.

Merry Christmas, my friends!
Ruthy

Get 4 FREE REWA...

We'll send you 2 FREE Books plus 2 FREE Mystery Gifts.

Love Inspired® Suspense books feature Christian characters facing challenges to their faith... and lives.

FREE Value Over $20

FREE REWARDS!

We'll send you 2 FREE Books plus 2 FREE Mystery Gifts.

Harlequin® Heartwarming™ Larger-Print books feature traditional values of home, family, community and—most of all—love.

FREE Value Over **$20**

READERSERVICE.COM

Manage your account online!

- Review your order history
- Manage your payments
- Update your address

> *We've designed the*
> *Reader Service website*
> *just for you.*

Enjoy all the features!

- Discover new series available to you, and read excerpts from any series.
- Respond to mailings and special monthly offers.
- Browse the Bonus Bucks catalog and online-only exculsives.
- Share your feedback.

Visit us at:
ReaderService.com